EXPLICIT ENCOUNTERS

EXPLICIT ENCOUNTERS

A collection of twenty erotic stories

Edited by Elizabeth Coldwell

Published by Xcite Books Ltd – 2011

ISBN 9781907761768

Printed and bound by CPI Group (UK) Ltd, Croydon, CR0 4YY

Cover design by Madamadari

Contents

MILF and Cookies
by Michael Bracken

The smell of fresh-baked chocolate chip cookies overpowered my senses when I entered the two-storey Colonial half a step behind my college roommate. Charlie Parker and I were spending Christmas break with his mother and I hadn't expected their home to be quite so grand nor had I anticipated the kind of homey touches I'd only previously seen on the movie screen.

I could see the living room from the foyer where we stood. A fully decorated Christmas tree dominated the room, stockings hung from the fireplace mantle, and Christmas knick-knacks seemed to be everywhere. Even the stairway leading to the second floor had silver garland strung through the banister supports.

'That you, Charlie?' When a slender woman wearing black slacks and a red sweater embellished with reindeer stepped into the foyer I closed my iPhone and slipped it into my pocket. Blonde hair cascaded in waves to her shoulders and her blue eyes glittered with amusement. Her lips were a slash of red that matched the polish on her long fingernails, and her figure would have been the envy of any college cheerleader. In fact, her sweater was stretched so tight across her ample bosom that Rudolph's nose seemed disproportionately large.

I envied the reindeer's proximity to such a bounteous bosom, and I almost swallowed my tongue when Charlie introduced me to his mother. My roommate and I are the same age – 21 – and his mother looked young enough to pass for Charlie's sister. I couldn't help myself. I had impure thoughts about Mrs Parker – even though I knew she was divorced, I couldn't help but think of my roommate's mother as "Mrs" – and felt my cock thicken as the thoughts became increasingly graphic.

Charlie nudged me, shaking me from my reverie. 'Our rooms are upstairs.'

Charlie's mother was still baking when I joined her in the kitchen after unpacking, and she had a warm, fresh-baked chocolate chip cookie in her hand. She broke off a small piece of the cookie and held it in front of my face. There was no way to get it from her without taking her fingers into my mouth and I hesitated.

'It's OK, Bobby,' she said. 'Take it.'

I leaned forward and wrapped my lips around her fingers, sucking the bite of cookie from between them. She slowly pulled her fingers away.

'Oh,' she said, 'you've left a bit of chocolate.'

She took her middle finger into her mouth and sucked off the chocolate. Then she said, 'Would you like another bite?'

Before I could respond, my roommate came clomping down the stairs. His mother winked and stepped away from me before Charlie entered the kitchen.

He grabbed one of the freshly baked cookies, bit it in half, and asked, 'When's dinner?'

'Six.'

'Then we have time,' Charlie said. He grabbed a handful of cookies and motioned for me to follow.

We spent the rest of the afternoon on a whirlwind tour of the town where Charlie had grown up, but I really didn't care about his high school or the various places he had hung out with his friends. I was still thinking about his mother and the sight of her middle finger as she slowly pulled it from between her lips.

In between Charlie's stories about drunken bashes with his friends and feeling up this girl or that girl, I learned that his parents had divorced when he was in high school and that, as far as he knew, his mother had not been involved with anyone since the divorce.

We returned to Charlie's house a few minutes before six, helped his mother set the dining room table, and then settled down for pot roast.

Mrs Parker asked about our classes, our professors, and our grades, and we answered her questions. Charlie did most of the talking because I had his mother's bare foot in my crotch, massaging my balls and my stiffening cock through the thick material of my jeans.

'You have a girlfriend yet, Charlie?' she asked her son.

'Nobody serious,' he told her.

She looked across the table at me. 'What about you?' she asked as her toes slid up the length of my erect cock. 'Are you dipping your cookies in any lucky girl's milk?'

I swallowed hard before answering. 'No, ma'am.'

She smiled.

We had finished our dinner by then, and Charlie pushed his plate aside. 'Let's see what's on the tube.'

I had no desire to stand while my cock was tenting the front of my jeans. 'In a minute,' I told him. To Mrs Parker, I said, 'Can I help with the dishes?'

She drew her foot out of my lap. 'That's OK, Bobby,' she said as she stood. 'I'll take care of the dishes.'

I waited for my cock to deflate while she gathered our plates and silverware and disappeared into the kitchen, and then I joined Charlie in the den where he'd found a tit-flick on Skinamax, and we watched movies until well past midnight.

Mrs Parker had gone to bed long before Charlie and I headed upstairs, so I was surprised to run into her when I came out of the bathroom. She stood in the doorway to her bedroom, more in shadow than not. The sash of her ankle-length white terrycloth robe wasn't pulled tight and an inch-wide gap revealed a short, gauzy red nightie underneath. She didn't appear to have anything on beneath the nightie. I wore a thin pair of sweat pants and I'm certain she could see the outline of my inflating cock through the material.

'It's going to be a long week, Bobby,' she said. 'A long, hard week.' She reached out and touched my cheek, letting her fingernail trail along my jaw line. 'I hope we'll be friends before the week is over.'

Charlie's door opened and his mother stepped back into the shadows of her bedroom.

'You done in the bathroom yet?' Charlie asked.

Mrs Parker shook the robe off her shoulders and let it drop to the floor. Moonlight filtering through the window behind Charlie's mother confirmed that she wore nothing beneath the nightie, then she pushed her bedroom door closed.

'Just finished,' I said.

Charlie and I crossed paths in the hall. He stepped into the bathroom and I put myself to bed in the guest room.

When I opened my eyes the next morning, I saw Charlie's mother standing in the doorway, holding a tray containing a glass of milk and a plate of chocolate chip cookies. She wore red spike heels and a red apron with a white snowman embroidered on it that hung from her neck and fastened around her waist. I blinked when I realised she wasn't wearing anything else.

'Charlie's father called and wanted to see him. He'll be away all morning,' she said. 'I thought you might like breakfast in bed.'

'Mrs Parker,' I said, 'you're trying to seduce me. Aren't you?'

'I've seen the movie, Bobby,' she said as she crossed the

4

room and put the tray on the nightstand. 'And you'd be correct.'

She broke off a piece of one of the cookies and pressed it between my lips until I had taken her middle finger all the way in and her palm cupped my chin. I sucked and sucked hard.

Using her free hand, Mrs Parker flipped back the covers, revealing the cock tent in my sweat pants. Then she slowly drew her finger from my mouth. She fed me another bite of cookie and then a third.

I tried to rise but she put a hand on my shoulder and pressed me back into the pillow. Then she climbed on the bed and straddled me. My stiff cock pressed against her thigh through the thin material of my sweat pants, but she wasn't interested in my cock. She slid upward until she had her hands pressed against the wall, her thighs around my ears, her apron draped over the top of my head, and her pussy poised above my mouth.

'I have something better for you to eat, Bobby,' she said. Then she lowered herself onto my face. Her curly blonde pussy hair tickled my nose while I licked her swollen pussy lips. I don't know what she'd been doing before she entered my room, but she was already wet with desire.

I slid my hands up, under the snowman, and cupped her breasts. I couldn't see them because her fuzzy quim covered half my face and the bottom of her apron covered the rest of my face, but I could feel them. They were firm and far more than a handful. Her constricted areolas were nubbly circles the size of half-dollars surrounding thick nipples that strained against my thumbs.

As I stroked her turgid nipples with the balls of my thumbs, I parted her outer pussy lips with my tongue and quickly found the tight bud of her swollen clit. I sucked it between my teeth and held it as I teased it with the tip of my tongue. Then I drove my tongue deep into her love hole, pulled it out and drove it in again several times between I returned my attention to her clit.

Mrs Parker ground her hips against my face, and the faster I licked her clit the faster her hips moved. She was so slick with desire that I had to swallow to keep from choking, and her womanly tang mixed intoxicatingly with the residue of chocolate remaining in my mouth from the cookies.

My roommate's mother arched her back and thrust her heavy breasts forward, pulling them from my hands. She suddenly stopped and cried out. I continued licking her clit until she shoved one hand under the apron and covered my mouth.

'Stop, Bobby, stop,' she urged between gasps for breath, and she didn't move until she caught her breath.

Then Mrs Parker slid down until she was sitting on my knees. When she grabbed the waistband of my sweats, I lifted my hips so she could pull them down to the middle of my thighs, revealing my erect cock and heavy balls. Under her breath, she said, 'Merry Christmas to me.'

Then she bent forward, took my swollen purple cockhead into her mouth, and wrapped her lips around my turgid cock shaft. As she wrapped one fist around the base of my cock, Mrs Parker licked away a drop of precome and then painted my cockhead with her saliva. I reached down and put my hands on the back of her head, intending to wrap my fingers in her long blonde hair and push her face into my crotch the way I did with the coeds I usually bedded. My roommate's mother batted my hands away and I took the hint.

She pumped her fist up and down my cock shaft as she continued painting my cockhead with her tongue. Before long my hips began moving up and down and my ball sack began to tighten. Mrs Parker must have sensed what was about to happen. She released her grip on my cock and buried her face in my crotch, taking my entire length into her oral cavity just as I came.

I fired thick gobs of hot come against the back of her throat. She swallowed every drop and held my cock in her mouth until it stopped spasming.

Then my roommate's mother shifted position and sat on the side of the bed. She reached for the glass of milk and washed down my come with one long drink. I pulled my sweat pants up and shifted position so I was sitting on the side of the bed next to Charlie's mother. Then she handed the milk glass to me. I drained it and put it back on the tray.

Mrs Parker stood, retrieved the tray, and carried it from the bedroom, giving me a great view of her firm, naked ass until she disappeared into the hall.

When Charlie returned home early that afternoon, he found his mother and me sitting in the living room near the Christmas tree drinking warm cider. I'd been helping her wrap a couple of last-minute gifts for my roommate and we had only just finished cleaning up the evidence. Charlie apologised for leaving me alone all morning and asked what I did for breakfast.

'I ate out,' I told him.

'My mom didn't fix you anything?' He turned toward his mother. 'Mom – '

I cut him short. 'Don't worry about it, Charlie,' I said. 'She took care of me this morning. I have no reason to complain.'

'What did your father want?' Mrs Parker asked.

'The usual,' Charlie told her. 'He gave me my Christmas present and then spent the rest of the morning complaining about his life without you.'

That was more information than I needed to hear, so I excused myself and went to the kitchen to find some cookies to snack on while they talked.

Nothing more significant than having another cookie hand-fed to me happened during the next few days because Charlie never left his mother and me alone for more than a few minutes. By the time Christmas Eve rolled around

Charlie's mother was willing to risk getting caught.

Shortly after we all went to our rooms, she opened my door and found me sitting up in bed, the lamp next to the bed providing just enough light for me to text holiday wishes to family and friends on my iPhone. She had her hair pulled back and held in place with a red holiday bow and she wore the robe I'd seen her wearing the first night. She let it slip off her shoulders and pool on the carpet at her feet.

This was the first time I had seen her completely naked and she was beautiful. Her radiant skin was smooth and unblemished, her constricted areolas and firm nipples wine dark against her pale skin. My cock responded to the sight. I propped my iPhone on the nightstand and rose to meet her as she crossed the room. I gathered her in my arms, felt her heavy breasts flatten against my chest, and covered her mouth with mine. We kissed long and deep, our tongues entwining in a fiery dance of desire.

She was naked but I wasn't. She forced one hand between us, under the waistband of my sweatpants, and took my thick cock in her hand and began stroking it.

'Santa Claus will be coming soon,' she whispered. 'What about you?'

I pushed my sweat pants down and stepped out of them. Then I took Charlie's mother in my arms again. I kissed her lips, her chin, and the hollow at the base of her throat. My lips trailed lower and I kissed one breast and then the other. I took one nipple in my mouth and sucked hard until it was fully erect. Then I did the same with her other nipple.

I slipped one hand between us, cupped her pussy in my palm and slid my middle fingers along her pussy slit. She opened to me and I slipped my fingers into her, quickly finding the tight button of her clit. I stoked it as I kissed my way back up to her mouth and fastened my lips on hers.

My fingers moved faster and faster. Soon her hips were thrusting back and forth, and I still had my mouth fastened on hers when she came. She mewled into my oral cavity as her quim quivered around my fingers and her legs grew weak.

I spun my roommate's mother around, bent her over the bed, and guided the head of my cock to her pussy opening where it nestled between her outer lips. Then I grabbed her hips and thrust forward, burying my cock deep inside her. I drew back and pressed forward again and again, banging her so hard her heavy breasts slapped forward and back.

I felt my nut sack tighten and knew I couldn't last any longer. I slammed into Charlie's mother one last time, driving my cock deeper than before, and then erupted within her, firing thick wads of hot come deep inside her still-quivering quim.

We stood like that for a minute or so, and then Mrs Parker pulled away, turned, and sat on the edge of the bed. She took my now-flaccid cock in her mouth and licked it clean.

My cock responded to her oral caresses and quickly regained its former stature. She sucked and sucked hard and soon I came a second time. When my cock stopped spasming in her mouth, Mrs Parker drew away, stood, and retrieved her robe from the floor. As she pulled it on, she said, 'Merry Christmas, Bobby.'

Then she slipped out of my room and left me to dream of chestnuts roasting on open fires. But first I turned off my iPhone.

I spent most of Christmas morning watching Charlie and his mother unwrap the gifts they had given one another, and, over a late morning snack of milk and cookies, I listened to Charlie's polite protestations that they hadn't gotten anything for me.

'It's OK,' I told my roommate as I smiled at his mother. 'I enjoyed coming here.'

'And I certainly enjoyed you coming,' his mother said. 'You're welcome to come again any time.'

Charlie looked at me, looked at his mother, and then shrugged, oblivious to the coded message we had exchanged.

When we left the next day, Charlie's mother walked us to the car. She waited until we were settled in our seats before rapping on my window. I rolled it down and she leaned in to talk to us. She wore a low-cut green sweater decorated with embroidered Christmas ornaments, and I could see deep into her cleavage.

'You two have plans for spring break?' she asked.

'Not yet,' Charlie replied.

'You're welcome to spend the week here,' she said.

Then she handed me a box containing fresh-baked chocolate chip cookies and winked. 'A little something to remember your visit.'

Mrs Parker didn't know it, but the cookies weren't the only mementos I was taking with me. I also had the recording I'd made with my iPhone on Christmas Eve.

I spent the entire trip back to school trying to figure out how to send Charlie to South Padre Island while I spent spring break alone with his mother.

Taking Her Out
by Penelope Friday

I know he's coming over this evening and I can hardly wait. It's tempting to touch myself and give myself a bit of much needed relief, but he's told me no, that I have to wait for him. And the bastard's capable of making me wait all night if necessary. I want him now. I want him more than now; I want him five minutes ago. I want to be naked and panting in his arms now, his mouth suckling my breast, making my nipple pointy and aching. I realise that my hand, despite my best intentions, has crept up and is playing with my left breast through my blouse. I am braless and knickerless tonight; all neat and decent formality on top and wanton sexuality underneath. The stockings, I think, are inspired: sheer and black, they could yet masquerade as utilitarian tights; one has to explore further to discover that they end, temptingly, halfway up my thigh.

But he has got me where he wants me now, hanging on his every move. I can't sit still; I'm up at the window every minute or so, peeping carefully through the curtains, thinking every car I hear passing might be his pulling in. I have to keep hidden behind the curtain as I watch: he's told me to be patient, to sit still like a good girl – when he knows that I want to be anything but good with him. He knows I want to rip his clothes off and sink to my knees in front of him, closing my mouth around his cock. And now I'm shifting in my seat, wondering whether I can hold on for him. My skirt reaches just above my knee, and I'm desperate to push my fingers under the hem and into the dampness between my legs.

I've just heard a car stop. Stop, not drive past. I realise my breathing is quick and shallow, that every muscle in my body is tense with anticipation. He turns the key in the door, and I find myself stroking the wrinkles out of my blouse, making certain my hair is just as I intend it.

'Leah?' His voice is deep; it sends shivers straight through me, all ending at the base of my spine, tingling through my clit.

'Here.'

He pushes open the door to the lounge, and I can see him, silhouetted by the light from the hall, standing in the doorway. He flips a switch and sets a tiny light ablaze, so that he can see me too. But I can't just see him, I can literally feel his presence.

'Have you been a good girl?' he demands.

I nod.

He strolls in, lazily, coming over to me and putting his hand on my cheek, turning my face up to his.

'What a pity,' he drawls. He looks me up and down. 'Oh,' he says, in a new tone, 'Oh, very smart. It seems a pity to stay in when you're dressed up so beautifully. I think I'll take you out.'

My jaw drops. He knows what I want, he knows precisely what is in my mind – it starts with "I'll take you" but doesn't end in "out". 'You ...?'

'Come on.' He pulls me gently to my feet, runs a possessive hand down my back until it lingers smoothly on my arse.

'But ...' I protest.

'A very nice butt,' he murmurs in my ear, his hand firming its hold.

He leads me to the door and walks me down the street toward the local pub. He has not even kissed me, I realise

12

with mounting indignation; and I halt him and rise on tiptoe to remedy this issue. Smiling, he puts a finger across my lips.

'You're supposed to be my good, patient girl,' he reminds me. I suck his finger into my mouth, swirling my tongue around it. 'You know,' he says quietly as we get to the pub door, 'I'm not so sure you're a good girl after all.'

'Oh, I am,' I assure him. 'I'm very good.'

'Hmm ...' He removes his finger and takes my hand. 'What do you want to drink?'

He orders, while I find a sofa in a dark corner of the room. When he comes over, he puts the drinks on the table and slides in next to me, his hand slipping down my leg from thigh to knee.

'What are you wearing, Leah?' he asks.

'You can see what I'm wearing,' I tell him demurely.

'Underneath?' he says.

'You can see just precisely what I'm wearing,' I say, and smile.

He leans over and takes the ridge of my ear in his mouth, biting gently before letting go.

'Definitely not a good girl,' he says. He does not sound displeased. 'And so ... if I were to run my fingers up your leg, Leah; if your skirt were to hitch up a little more, what would I find? Are you wet, Leah, waiting for me? Do you want me to slide my fingers inside you, to stroke your clit with my thumb?' I am wriggling in my seat now, shifting from side to side. I'm not so much wet as soaked, and my pulse – my extremely fast pulse – seems to have taken up residence in my lower abdomen. 'For shame, Leah,' he chides me. 'We're in public; you must control yourself.'

I glare at him and take a bigger than intended sip of my wine. It does nothing to cool me down from the sweat he has me in, as he is well aware. His hand is sideways across my knee, his fingers slipping into the crack between my legs and moving with a gentle, insistent pressure. I squeeze my legs together, trapping his hand.

'Jay!'

'Mmm.'

He smiles at me, damn him. I wonder whether anyone has ever died of unfulfilled lust, and swear to myself I'll take him with me if it's going to happen. I pick up my drink, curling my fingers around the glass stem with deliberate slowness.

'Thank you for the wine,' I say politely.

My eyes on his, I raise the glass to my lips, taking a mouthful of deep, mellow, merlot into my mouth. My tongue traces my lips as I savour the taste – the taste both of the wine and of rebellion; of making him feel a little of what he does to me. He presses my leg firmly, and disentangles his hand, running the tip of his index finger down my arm from shoulder to wrist.

'My pleasure,' he says.

He cups both of his palms around his pint, rolling it between his hands as he has done so often before with my breasts. I am a rank amateur in comparison with him, and he knows it. He knows it, and oh, does he use it! I squeeze my legs even tighter together, and wonder whether it's possible to come without being touched, without even touching myself. When I try and pick my wine glass up again, my hand is shaking slightly. He sees, of course.

'Nervous, Leah?'

'No.' Damn him, he knows I'm not nervous. He knows I'm desperate.

He smiles and changes the subject. 'Beautiful weather there's been today, hasn't there?' he says in a conversational tone. 'Dry, warm – just what you want and so rarely get in an English summer.'

He is trying to provoke me. He *must* be trying to provoke me. He must know that I don't give a damn about the weather. 'Mm,' I say, glaring at him.

'Hot, one might even call it. Doesn't it heat you inside,

Leah; isn't there a warm glow flushing through your body? Do you feel the sweat clinging to your skin, nestling between your breasts?' He runs one finger around the neckline of my blouse. 'You seem hot,' he comments.

'It's the pub,' I say through gritted teeth. 'I'm sure I'd be better if we went elsewhere. Home, maybe?'

He shakes his head. 'But we've only just come out. You haven't finished your drink yet.'

I scowl, and down the rest of the wine in one gulp. 'Now can we go home?'

'Leah!' he chides. 'I've got a lot of my drink left. You shouldn't rush these things, you know – take time to savour it. Now, you see, you have nothing to do but sit and watch me.'

I know he won't hurry. He'll probably drink even more slowly as a punishment for my daring to object.

'I might get another drink,' I say.

He puts a hand on my arm. 'If you wish.' I can tell from his tone that I would be wise not to carry through. Besides, if I am honest, I don't want another drink. I didn't want the first. I want him, and he's going to make me wait as long as he chooses. 'Sultry,' he murmurs; then, as I look at him, 'The weather, dear girl. Positively sultry.'

'There's a breeze,' I say, for something to say.

'Oh, but don't you think ...' He is speaking in a lower tone now, just above a whisper. His voice is mesmerising. 'Don't you think it is just the weather for lying in the evening dusk, underneath a tree? The breeze could tickle your skin, but I could make sure you kept warm.' He slides his hand up my leg again, pushing up my skirt to an almost indecent level. I have to use all my willpower in order not to slide down in the seat so that his fingers can trail through my wetness and dive inside me. 'What do you think, Leah?' he asks again.

'I think ...' I stop, and unable to resist any longer, lean across and kiss him firmly on the mouth.

'Oh, now!' he laughs. 'Patience, remember.'

'Patience.' I nod, as if what he's said is quite reasonable, and smooth my skirt down, gathering his hand up in mine. 'Patience,' I say again, sucking his forefinger into my mouth and letting my tongue tease its way around it before letting it go. 'I've got a lot of patience,' I say, repeating the gesture. 'A lot.' I do it for the third time, and looking down, I can see that I am having an effect on him. 'So,' I say, leaning on the table, knowing that my breasts are outlined through my blouse, 'do you come often?'

He raises an eyebrow.

'Here, I mean,' I say innocently. 'Do you come here often?'

'I don't think,' and his voice is deeper, throatier, 'that I've ever come here. But I'm tempted to tonight.'

'The facilities are good,' I agree. 'A nice bar ...' I lower my voice. 'And an even nicer garden area. I think you'd like it.'

'Show me.'

I slide out of my seat and hold a hand out to him. 'This way.'

He takes my hand. 'I am in your hands,' he murmurs.

'Not yet,' I say, 'but you will be. And my mouth.' We open the door to the pub garden, and I add, 'It's often rather empty out here – not many of the customers come this way. The bar staff do, occasionally ...'

His hand has found its way right underneath my skirt; his palm is warm on my arse. 'I never knew you were such an exhibitionist, Leah. Does the thought that we might be caught turn you on?'

'*You* turn me on,' I reply, pulling him into my arms and pressing myself against him. 'The thought of having you anywhere turns me on.'

He nuzzles the side of my neck, and bites gently on my ear. 'But admit it,' he whispers, 'you're getting a thrill out of the risk, aren't you?'

And maybe ... just maybe he has a point. I unbuckle his jeans and slip my hand inside his pants, and part of the swift beating of my heart is because at the same time I'm looking around, wondering whether anyone will see us, wondering what they'd do if they did. There's quite a sexy-looking barman here; what would he think if he saw us? Would he be outraged, ban us from the pub forever, maybe call the police? Or would he get a kick out of watching us, wishing that the bar was empty so that he could wank over the sight? But Jay is unbuttoning my blouse and lowering his mouth to my nipple, and it is impossible to think of any man but he. I arch my back, and the branches on the tree we are under catch in my hair and tug at it like hands. He picks me up and positions me with my back against the tree. I curl my legs around his hips, grinding against him. Jay doesn't bother to undress further, but slips inside me, pushing me back against the rough bark, and pressing a hand across my mouth as I moan my pleasure.

'Quiet,' he warns. 'You don't want the world to know what a naughty, wanton girl you are, do you?'

But I am not interested in conversing now, not with his cock buried deep inside me. I undulate my hips, pulling him further in and then releasing him a little. Jay laughs, and this time accepts my wordless plea, his mouth crushing mine in a kiss which is a mark of his possession. He knows what turns me on. He knows I am his, whenever and wherever he chooses to take me. And he chooses now.

I have no time for words, no inclination for thought, even. The idea that we might be seen flits through my brain, lost under the clamour of my body, which is crying out for Jay, desperate to be taken further and further down the path which only he knows. He is gentle and rough alternately, demanding and giving all at once. I am biting my lip in order to keep my silence; a tear runs hotly down my cheek, but I have no hand with which to brush it away. My hands will only concentrate on him. And ...

17

'Come on, now,' he whispers. 'Come, Leah – come.'

It is as if I can do nothing but obey. My body spasms gloriously around him; my eyes are squeezed shut and more colours, more feelings than the world can possibly imagine dance in my brain, fizzing through my nerves and making me gasp for breath, my forehead resting on Jay's shoulder. I feel him pulse inside me; he gives the small moan which is the only sound he makes as he comes. For a moment we stay still, locked into each other's bodies; and then, gently, he lowers me to my feet.

'Jay – Jay!' I repeat his name over and over.

He smiles, buttoning up his trousers, smoothing my skirt over my hips. 'Not such a good girl, after all,' he says, his voice satisfied. 'And do you know, Leah, I rather like you that way.'

Deeds of Mercy
by Giselle Renarde

If Mercedes had to sum up her ridiculously complex sex life, it would go something like this: she used to date an older guy named Simon, who was all the while married to a woman called Florence. After years of hope and heartbreak, Mercedes broke it off with Simon and ultimately found herself engaged to a young guy named Anwar. Things were pretty solid until Mercedes met up with Simon again, purely by chance. She had no intention of hooking up with him ... until he made her an offer of cold, hard cash! With Mercedes' love of secrets, cocks, and infidelity, how could she refuse?

Mercedes' romantic world had grown into a man-eating monstrosity. She pictured it looking a lot like that giant plant from *Little Shop of Horrors*. She couldn't say why she kept seeing Simon. She really did love Anwar. It wasn't that she needed the money. Well, OK, the money was nice and it gave her a cheap thrill every time she added Sex-with-Simon cash to the Wedding-with-Anwar fund, but it's not like she was living at subsistence level. She didn't *need* it. But she liked it. She enjoyed the naughty thrill of prostituting herself to her married ex-lover while her husband-to-be remained oblivious.

Simon was very different as a paying customer than he'd been back when Mercedes was simply his doting mistress. He'd been so careful before. Now he took all sorts of chances. He didn't seem to give a fuck about getting caught. Maybe that was a product of now being able to say, 'What, this chick? I'm just paying her to suck my balls. Don't feel threatened, wifey.' Mercedes was sure the money made all the difference.

In the four years of their "couplehood", such as it was, Mercedes had never seen Simon's house. Never. She'd never seen his wife or his grown children, live in person or via any other medium. They'd been names, nothing more. In fact, his entire family was off-limits to her, though the rule itself remained unspoken.

That was then. Now, when Florence left town to visit her relatives for the weekend, Simon insisted Mercedes stay the night.

'At your house?' she asked.

'At my house,' he replied.

'But ...' Mercedes couldn't seem to locate the words required to express her trepidation. She wasn't even sure what precisely she was worried about. 'A whole night? That's ... a lot of hours. And we'll be ... sleeping together?'

Even over the phone, Simon sounded peeved. 'The whole time we were together, you begged me to spend the night with you. Now you don't want to?' He let out a *humph* and then said, 'I'll pay you per hour of sleep, if that's what you're so worried about.'

'No, no. I mean, yes, thank you, but ...' It finally clicked why she shouldn't be spending nights with her ex. 'Anwar! What am I supposed to tell Anwar?'

'Are you suddenly living together?' Simon asked in his rhetorical voice. 'No? Then what difference does it make where you sleep?'

Setting emotion aside, Mercedes looked at the situation from a business perspective: she could either spend Saturday night falling asleep in front of Anwar's TV, or go to Simon's house, get fucked, get paid, go to sleep, get paid, and probably get fucked and paid once again come morning.

'Okay,' she said. 'You're right. I'll make it work.'

With a simple lie about a girls' night, Mercy set off to visit Simon's house for the first time. Her stomach tied itself in knots. She felt strange, knowing she'd be fucking some woman named Florence's husband in said woman named Florence's house. She felt sleazy about it. *Florence*. What an old lady name. Who was this woman named Florence? And why had Mercedes never wondered about her before now? Why did Simon cheat? Did this woman drive him to it? Was she horrible? Demeaning? Lame-o in bed? That must be it. Why else would Simon pay Mercedes for sex?

When she arrived at his door, Mercy expected Simon to grab her by the arm and swoop her inside, whispering, 'Did the neighbours see you?' Well, that isn't how it went down. Simon opened the door, casting a dark shadow across the stoop. He looked her up and down. Even as a dog-walking couple sauntered along the sidewalk, Simon smiled and told her she looked good enough to eat.

'I hope so,' she mumbled as she crept inside.

She thought she'd be curious about this house of Simon's, but her present feeling was exactly the opposite of curiosity. Mercedes tried not to look anywhere or see anything. Her senses dulled as he guided her by the arm. She stared down at her stocking feet against dark hardwood floors. Where were her shoes? She must have taken them off without realising.

There were pictures on the walls, but Mercedes wouldn't allow herself to look at them, not even to distinguish whether they were paintings of photographs. Why had she come here? Business, pleasure, or pure masochism?

Soon, they came to be in a bedroom on the second floor of the house. When had they ascended a staircase? Mercy's mind was muddled with desire for absentia intermingled with desire for Simon. Despite her best efforts to find the man unattractive, she couldn't help being drawn to a body that defied age. Simon was always hard before his pants hit

21

the ground, and his erections were thick and firm. When he fucked her, she always left satisfied. Better than satisfied, in fact ... Swollen and wet, sore and gasping for breath.

Now he seemed to be undressing her. No, scratch that. He seemed to have *undressed* her. Mercy's clothing hung over the back of a chair by the wooden desk. He was undressed too, but his clothes were on the floor. As always, his erection shot out in front of him like it was dowsing for wetness. Yes, Mercy realised, she was dripping for him. *Dripping*.

Simon's hard cock swung side to side as he strutted to the bedroom door and closed it. His body gleamed golden in the low light of two bedside lamps, which cast Mercy's shadow up against the adjacent wall. The room was stark, she noticed. But she didn't want to notice – anything – so she focused her attention on Simon. 'How do you want me?' she asked.

He could do anything to her. They'd agreed on a flat rate for any activity, except for the hours of sleep, which would cost extra. He usually started with a blowjob and finished off fucking her pussy. On rare occasions he fucked her ass, but he knew that hurt her and she really didn't like it all that much.

'I want to eat you,' he said. His forceful gaze burned like the glowing embers in the gas fireplace across from the bed. 'I miss the taste of your cunt. I want you on my tongue.'

That statement should have excited her, but Mercy was too entranced by the fireplace. It seemed brand new. Why would a couple with a lousy sex life get a gas fireplace installed in their bedroom? It wouldn't be for heat. There were plenty of other ways to heat up a bedroom. *God!* Simon and his wife couldn't possibly have a healthy sex life, could they? If they did, why did Simon have an affair with Mercedes? Why was he now paying her for the pleasure of eating her pussy? But what reason other than romance was there for a new fireplace in a bedroom?

Simon lifted her off her feet and dropped her on the bed. She bounced. The quilt was too pretty to mess up with her juices, but it was too late now. As Simon crawled up from the base of the bed, snarling like a wild thing, Mercy felt her inner thighs drench with juice. She crept back from him and drowned in a multitude of pillows. There was nowhere left to go. Only a wooden headboard remained at her back. Simon smiled in a sneering sort of way. 'Where are you going, Mercy? I thought you wanted me to eat you.'

'I do,' she said. Her heart fluttered as he grabbed her ankles and pulled her legs wide open.

'Nice work if you can get it,' he teased as he propelled his body between her legs like a trench soldier. 'You just sit back and enjoy my tongue on your pussy, and then you go home with your bra stuffed with cash. Wish I could find a job like that.'

His smugness would have pissed her off a few years ago. Now it turned her on. She couldn't bring herself to play the possession. 'It's too late for you,' she replied. 'Gotta be young and beautiful for a sweet position like this.'

'Sweet position?' Simon chuckled as he dove between her thighs. He went right at it and obviously didn't plan on letting up until she came hard enough to wake the neighbours. Back when they were a "couple", he'd been so dainty about eating her. He'd give her clit a few licks, she'd pretend he was God's gift, and then they'd move on to something else.

This was something else altogether. Simon was like a different person now that he was paying for sexual gratification. He tore into her like a beast. Holding her thighs wide apart, he pressed his face firm against her pussy so his lips met her clit and his nose planted in her trimmed bush. Mercy could feel the stubble on his chin against the base of her wet slit. His bristled cheeks scratched her outer lips like pleasant sadists as he took her clit in his hot mouth.

Mercy's whole body jumped. Simon sucked her clit like

it was a tiny cock. This was something she'd never experienced before. Where had Simon picked up new material? Was it something his wife had taught him? No, couldn't be. Mercy was convinced they had next to no sex life. She'd convinced herself.

Sensation melted Mercy's mind. She bucked against Simon's face. Now she knew why guys got off on blowjobs. As Simon sucked her inner lips in with her clit, she tossed her head back and grabbed his with both hands. She thrust her hips at his face until she felt the scratch of his whiskers against her slit. His nose was flush to her bush. Could he even breathe down there? Mercy didn't give a fuck. She ran her pussy in tight circles against his muzzle. The prickle against her tender flesh generated an itch to fuck, and she hoped he'd get his cock inside her soon.

She'd have to come first, of course, but that was no chore. The harder Simon sucked her clit, the harder it became to resist giving herself over to the looming wave of climax. She forced her clit into his mouth, nearly sitting upright as he splayed himself belly-down on the bed. With his head in her hands, she pushed his face against her pussy the way porn star men do to porn star women when they're getting their blowjobs. She felt almost guilty to treat him this way, especially when he'd be paying her in the morning, but she was so close to coming she couldn't stop now.

Finally, the urge to move was subsumed by the urge to receive pleasure. Mercy held Simon's face against her pussy and screamed as he sucked her like mad.

When she finished screaming and could take no more pleasure or pain, Mercy closed up her legs and fell back into the cluster of pillows. Either her eyes were closed or she'd just gone blind. Her orgasm had so overtaken her she couldn't figure out which was the case. She finally realised her eyes were indeed closed, and she decided to open them. When she did, she saw two things: Simon looming between her knees with his long cock looking like it wanted to get up inside her, and, on the mantle behind him, a wedding photo. She must only have spent a few seconds looking at it, but she recognised a youthful Simon as the groom. The woman in the white gown was obviously his bride.

Mercy was shocked by this photo. Not because it was a wedding photo – she obviously knew Simon was married. This photo told her one thing she'd never known about the man: his wife was pug fugly. Worse than pug fugly! She had a face like a bulldog after a bar brawl. And in her wedding photo! A woman always looked her best on her wedding day. If Florence looked like that when she was married, imagine what she must look like now!

'I want to fuck you,' Simon growled. Slipping off the bed, he flipped her from her back to her front. 'I want it doggy style.'

'Yeah.' She felt too distracted to sound sexy. Then her gaze fell to another photo. This one sat on the night table right beside Mercy's face. It was definitely Florence – the face was an older, more wrinkled, an even uglier version of the one on the mantle. She looked like a Halloween hag. Could this really be Simon's wife? Christ, no wonder he was willing to pay Mercedes for sex!

As Mercy lay staring at the figure in the photo, Simon climbed on the bed and splayed her legs as far apart as they would go. That action jolted her into the moment. Her pussy clenched in anticipation. She closed her eyes, but the image of Simon's ugly wife seemed burnt into her retinas.

When Simon grabbed her hips, Mercy raised her ass to him. He knew exactly what he wanted these days, and he lifted her up to the perfect height. After piling up pillows under her pelvis, he wasted no time going at her. He rammed her so hard it panged inside, but Mercy didn't care. The pang of a gleaming purple cockhead against her insides hurt less than the sting of resentment in knowing what Simon had stayed with throughout their years together.

He scratched her back with sharp little nails as he fucked

her pussy. The pain felt wonderful. He smacked her ass cheeks until they turned red. That felt even better. But why had Simon stayed with such an ugly woman when he could have had Mercedes? As his cock raced in and out of her hot, wet pussy, Mercy realised how ridiculously narcissistic she was being. Maybe Florence was the nicest, sweetest, most internally beautiful person in the world! Maybe Simon had a thousand reasons to stay married to her.

Grunting like a troll, Simon threw his sweating chest on top of Mercy's back. The pillows piled underneath her pelvis held their butts aloft, but Simon grasped her wrists and held them down as he fucked her. She felt trapped in his body now, as her mind was trapped in a cycle of, 'Why her and not me? Why choose ugly when he could have beautiful? What's so great about Florence?'

Even as Simon grabbed Mercy's breasts and groaned, the pleasure of fucking couldn't dispel the multitude of questions. Simon propelled his hips at Mercy's ass and bit down hard on her shoulder. Mercy screeched. Pain soared through her body. Her blood sizzled in her veins. She was sweating all over this pretty marriage quilt, and her pussy juice now graced a stack of throw pillows. As her cunt clamped down on Simon's orgasmic cock, a series of words tumbled out of her mouth unhindered: 'My God, Simon, your wife is one pug ugly motherfucker!'

The room went silent as Simon rolled off Mercy's back. The bed bounced beneath them. Was there any utterance crueller than the one that had just passed through her lips? She'd insulted Simon's wife! This was the woman he'd been married to for how many years? And Mercy called her ugly. Why would she say that? Was she jealous? Even with her engagement to Anwar, was she still subconsciously coveting Simon? Was she still in love with him? Or was this wife of his simply unconscionably ugly?

'God, I know she is,' he finally said. 'And she always was. It's embarrassing, isn't it?'

With a growl, Simon pulled Mercedes down from her Princess-and-the-Pea stack of pillows. Tossing her onto her back, he rolled on top. His spent cock drooled forgotten spurts of come against her leg as he took her breast in his mouth and sucked. Everything he did to her was animalistic now. There was an intangible sort of brutality in his every move.

After a moment of vicious nipple sucking, Mercedes asked, 'Why did you marry her?'

Simon pressed Mercedes' breasts together. When he spoke, his voice resonated from somewhere inside her cleavage. 'Back in the day, she used to be great in the sack.' He laughed, and collapsed beside her on the bed. Grabbing a pillow for his head, he squeezed her in close to his body and closed his eyes. 'Same reason I stick with you.'

Mercy's heart froze in her chest. When Simon pressed a cruel kiss against her temple, she tried to ease herself away, but he only wrapped her tighter in his arms. The implications were too many, and too jarring. Her mind raced. Sure, he was paying her to stay the night, but Mercedes didn't sleep a wink.

Ghost
by Kay Jaybee

He was everywhere. At least, the logo of the stationery company he worked for was everywhere. There was no escape.

She hadn't expected the knock at the door. She'd hoped it would come, but she hadn't expected it. If Jo was honest with herself, too much of her time had been wasted longing for the sound of his distinctive hammering against the letterbox. As it wasn't a noise she'd heard for nearly three months, she'd almost resigned herself to it being merely a dream – a pointless hope. Almost. He was merely a shadow. A ghost. A ghost who was married to someone else. A ghost she had no right to see anyway.

Many had been the night, dildo in hand, her fingers straying over her body, eyes tightly closed, pretending he was there, planning how she would treat him if he ever showed up on her doorstep again expecting a fuck. Jo never dreamt she'd have the courage to actually go through with it, but then she'd never dreamt she was the sort of woman who had affairs until she met him. Sam Peters had changed everything.

Now, there he stood, all brown eyes, half smile and arrogant self-assurance, looking exactly as he always did, and resentment at all those wasted seconds; of every moment of disappointment when the knock at the door turned out to be another visitor entirely swept over Jo.

Saying nothing, she let him follow her into the cluttered living room. The door safely shut behind them, Sam immediately reached out, twisting Jo at the waist so she faced him, slipping his arms around her, murmuring, 'So how've you been?' into her neck as he kissed her, his stubble lightly grazing her skin.

His mouth moved to find hers, and Jo's resolve wavered for a moment as she inhaled the aroma of hard work that always hung around him. This was a man continuously in a hurry, rushing from one delivery to another, one quotation session to the next, and the telltale scent of sweat and deodorant lingered around him. Biting down her instant desire, Jo calmly replied, 'I'm good thanks. You?'

'Better now.' He led her to the end of her sofa and sat down, indicating for her to sit on his lap. Jo resisted, and remained standing, staring at his shining eyes for a moment, before kneeling and yanking off his grubby white trainers.

All the time she maintained eye contact with Sam, the weeks of neglect her body had felt driving her on. He was studying her in return, openly curious. Usually she'd be naked by now, doing whatever his body demanded of her in the few minutes they had before he had to rush off toward his next appointment.

Forcing herself not to wonder how much time Sam had, and if he was already ticking off the seconds until work required him to leave, Jo, wishing she'd known he was coming so that she wasn't just wearing her tatty jeans and sloppy black jumper, mentally took a deep breath. 'Take off your trousers and turn round.'

Grinning at her, Sam opened his mouth to speak, about to make a joke about her being in charge for a change, but she placed a finger against his lips. 'Just do it.' Although his eyebrows raised, displaying the devilish eyes that had first taken her down the road to becoming his mistress, he said nothing, and did as she asked.

'Good. Now lose the boxers, get on your knees, and lean

over the edge of the sofa.' She didn't wait to see if he obeyed, but walked away, climbing the stairs two at a time to retrieve the black canvas bag she kept under her bed, relieved that she'd managed to keep her voice steady and authoritative.

On her return, Jo paused by her desk, her gaze falling on the long plastic ruler she'd been using prior to his arrival to underline boring figures on a boring spreadsheet.

'Perfect.' She spoke out loud, referring to both the acquisition of the ruler, and the sight of Sam's naked arse bent over the sofa cushions.

Flipping open her bag of sex toys, Jo retrieved her latest purchase, a tiny pink vibrating bullet that had given her an immense amount of pleasure in the months since he'd last been there. Hiding it in her fist, she knelt behind Sam, wrapping her arms around his waist and, just as she'd pictured in her fantasy, slowly slipped her hands down to his rigid dick. Leaning forward so she could whisper in his ear, Jo let her fingers stray between his balls, teasing the hair that surrounded them. 'I think, young man; that it's high time you were taken in hand.

'Now I hope you're listening to me, because this is important.' Sam groaned in agreement as she wrapped the fist containing the bullet around his shaft. 'I try and get on with my life. I *do* live a life, but every day, every fucking day I see signs of you. Reminders of you are just *everywhere*!'

With a sharp flick, Jo activated the bullet, and felt the satisfying reaction of his surprised yelp as she trailed the powerful toy up and down his dick. Abruptly, Jo pulled her bullet away, making Sam moaned with loss for a split second, before she began to glide it back up his body, while her free hand searched out the ruler she'd slid into her bag.

'I go to the supermarket and I see us buying those trainers you wear ...' SMACK. 'I walk through the town, and adverts for the company you work for haunt me like

31

bloody ghosts ...' SMACK. 'I stand in this room and images of you, dressed, naked, gasping as I suck your cock ...' SMACK '... drive me to distraction ...'

Sam's only response to this catalogue of crimes was to sigh as his body rippled with lust between the cracks of the ruler and the glorious pressure of the powerful buzzer Jo had pushed inside his T-shirt, letting it tickle his chest hairs.

'You've changed me. I was so quiet, so very well behaved ...' SMACK. '... I would never have dreamt of spanking anyone, of being spanked, of shagging in the open air, of fucking someone else's husband for heaven's sake! You've changed me! You are *everywhere*!'

Clicking the vibrator on to full power while she caught her breath, her chest heaving, Jo was suddenly aware of how fast she'd been talking, and that she'd been virtually shouting. Slamming the bullet against his right nipple, making Sam whine, Jo threw back her arm and hit his arse even harder, turning the pink marks she'd already made red. '... And yet I *never* see you. All I get is ghosts. Reminders of where you once stood ...' SMACK. '... Of where you once licked me out; of where I stood while you ripped all my clothes off so fast, they were nothing but rags by the time you'd finished with me.' SMACK.

'And you won't even let me call you on your mobile; I can't even text you. I'm cut off ...' SMACK. '... And *I hate it*!'

Her breathing shallow, her throat arid, her arm aching, Jo cursed herself for going too far. Saying too much. She hadn't meant to mention the phone thing. She knew damn well it was risky to use it; her calls and texts were easy to trace, especially as Sam was useless at deleting things properly. He didn't want his wife finding out about them, and neither did she. It wasn't as if she wanted him all to herself or anything; this was just sex. She really didn't want to cause trouble – but for fuck's sake! How can you have any kind of affair with a man you can't contact and rarely see?

Three months of longing to feel his body against hers, his pulse hammering on her skin, was screaming at the back of her head. All the frustration of waiting now seemed to be centred between her legs. Jo knew she'd need some attention of her own soon.

Dropping the ruler, Jo eased the bullet speed down to slow, and ran it back to his balls, while she teased a digit over his anus. Tensing herself for him to be angry with her, for him to explain for the hundredth time why they couldn't keep in touch while he worked away, Jo was surprised when he turned round and buried his face in her neck, his tone subdued, as he murmured, 'Oh hell, babe, I can't. I ...'

Then something in her lover snapped. Sam threw off his T-shirt, and exhaled deeply, his dick quivering before him, pointing at her accusingly, 'Look, it's the same for me, all this ghost crap.' He scooped up the ruler, and with an anger born of his own frustration, a frustration Jo hadn't realised he shared, flipped her around, so that before she registered what was happening, their roles had been reversed.

Striking her buttocks through her denim jeans, Sam grunted, and swiftly looped his arms around her waist, undid her button fly, and dragged them to her ankles. Pausing to briefly smooth the black satin underwear he found beneath, he shoved her knickers down to join her trousers, and set about creating a pattern of his own against her pale backside.

'Yes!' She exhaled her pleasure into the soft sofa fabric as the plastic rebounded off her arse.

Discarding the ruler, Sam lifted his hand high into the air instead. As his skin connected with Jo's flesh, she yelled out in delight and amazement at how he always managed to make her burn with pain, and yet increase her longing for him.

'The ruler isn't hard enough for you is it. You're such a bad girl.' He aimed again. 'My bad girl, being spanked by another woman's man. You love it, don't you?' He aimed again, his palm beginning to burn in sympathy with her buttocks, as Jo flushed with shame at the truth of his words. She did love it. It was the only thing she'd ever done wrong in her life, the only time she was ever truly out of control, and she couldn't bear the thought of it ending.

'Well I'll tell you something, my little bitch.' Their skin connected again, his cruel words fuelling her arousal as much as her beating, 'You think you're the only one who sees ghosts? I see you all over the fucking place ...' SLAP '... I see you in the back of the van, positioned on all fours, begging me to spear you. There are houses that look like your home all over the place ...' SLAP '... but only behind your front door do I find you, all moist and waiting, always ready for a sex, always thinking filthy thoughts.'

Slipping a hand between her legs, he began to rub at her clit, smearing her juices into her skin, watching with satisfaction as her hips twitched and rose toward him. As he slammed his palm down on Jo again, her shrieks muted by the cushions, her arms stretched out behind her, she became desperate to grab hold of him, to feel his warm flesh, but she was unable to quite reach as Sam continued in his work.

'I wank at the images of you in my head every bloody day, and every flipping night I have to sneak out of bed to the bathroom and sort myself out. Sometimes I have to stop the van and yank off in the nearest field or toilets or somewhere, just to have some relief from the thought of what your body does to me.'

Whimpering with the tingling heat of her butt, tears gathering at the corners of her green eyes as the pain accelerated, yet smiling broadly into the cushions as she listened, Jo replied, 'I'm the same. Why do you think I bought that bullet? I can hardly carry a full-sized bunny dildo around in my handbag, can I?'

Sam laughed, a picture of Jo scuttling off to the toilets halfway through her supermarket shopping, pressing herself against a cubicle door as she thought about him turning him on further. His voice hoarse now, the anger of desire and her failure to understand that her frustration was shared, began to subside. 'I've been thinking a lot about this phone thing.'

Smacking her one last time, he bent and licked his tongue slowly over the reddening blotches that were blossoming across her arse.

'I can't have you using my private mobile. It's too risky.' He moved his thumb over her nub, as if to cut off her chance to interrupt him. 'But how about you becoming a customer?'

Her confusion at his suggestion was morphed into a nerve fluttering sigh as he eased two fingers up inside her snatch, all fleeting thoughts of re-seizing control and punishing him further, of tying him up and making him beg her to come, of forcing him to promise to banish all the ghosts, were forgotten as he pushed her toward climax.

Shoving his free hand up her shirt, Sam manoeuvred her swollen chest from her bra, making Jo cry out with liberation as he rolled her left nipple between firm, squeezing fingers.

'If you were a customer, your number could be entered on my work phone, and no one would ask why.'

Jo's mouth was too dry to respond; his pinching had moved to her other nipple, and she could feel the muscles in her stomach clench and tighten as the first wave of orgasm gathered within her.

Understanding how near she was, Sam pumped his fingers against Jo's mound, placing his thumb over her clit, and simultaneously kneading her chest. Jo pushed back against him, warm waves of jolting pleasure surging through her, leaving her panting into the furniture.

Only when her body had totally stilled, did Sam move away, lifting a stray red hair from her cheek. Helping Jo to her feet, he stared into her sparkling eyes. 'I know you don't need a single thing my company has to offer. But we could pretend you do.'

'How?' Jo already badly wanted this to work, but couldn't see how anyone would believe she needed to bulk order stationery of any sort.

'You could book me to give you quotes for paper. I could come over and discuss things, and then you could decide against making an order, then you could change your mind and invite me to come and give you a revised quote, and so on. It wouldn't be such a strange thing for you to do; you work from home, after all. Once your number is logged, no one will question it. I have numbers from clients I've not seen in years on the van phone.'

Jo ran a fingernail over his chin, the other playing with the hairs on his chest she loved so much. 'If it's that damn easy, why didn't you think of it before?'

'Because I'm an idiot; and because every time I come here, all normal, sensible and rational thoughts go out of my head.'

Jo swept off her remaining clothes and wrapped her arms around him. 'Sounds a fair answer. You certainly screw my head up – not to mention the rest of me. I was such a good girl until you came along.'

Abruptly Sam picked her up. Looping her legs around his waist, Jo clung on to him, as he roughly thumped her against the nearest wall, driving his dick into her.

Digging her nails into his shoulder, not caring about the questions his wife might ask him later as to where they had come from, Jo kissed him furiously as he thrust hard, filling her to the hilt, before almost totally withdrawing, then refilling her achingly desperate hole.

Coming quickly, Sam poured spunk into her like hot foam. 'Hell, I've missed you.'

Still entangled, they crashed down onto the sofa. 'So, are you up for being a customer?'

'You bet!'

'Oh thank God, because you really are everywhere you know. You're around every corner, in every thought. *You* are the ghost, Jo.' Sam sighed as he stroked her hair. 'I love my wife, but you, you're just so fucking ...'

Jo stopped him mid sentence by placing a hand over his. 'I know. We're like those people who meet over the Internet just to have an affair, except we happen to be friends too.' She smiled. 'I need you. I need us, like this, all lust and fantasy, but no more than that. More would ruin it. I *need* what we have – I just need it far more often!'

'Is that Jo Sanders?'

'Yes. Can I help you?'

'This is Sam Peters of *Stationery on the Move*. I believe you wish me to come and show you some samples and discuss some quotes?'

'Please. I am particularly interested in your reams of A4 paper, and an estimate of how long you think it might take for you to come once I have your cock down my throat?'

'I'm sure I can provide answers to those queries, madam. May I take some details?'

'Certainly.'

'Do you prefer to be spanked or bitten?'

'Spanked.'

'Licked out or to provide a blowjob?'

'Tough call, but licking out would have the edge.'

'So, perhaps we at *Stationery on the Move* could provide you with a quote for a sixty-nine as a suitable compromise?'

'That sounds excellent. Can I book a sixty-nine today, please, if you're in the area?'

'I'll be there in ten minutes, and for fuck's sake, be naked. I have a hard-on that makes your ruler look limp!'

'Yes, sir! Let yourself in, and follow the sound of the vibrator ...'

Making the Most of All in New Zealand
by Eva Hore

I was visiting my cousin in New Zealand. She'd promised me at her wedding if I ever came out they'd take me out and show me the sights. She's married to an extremely good-looking Maori guy, rugged, with chiselled features and a torso rippling with muscles like a body builder's.

The moment I laid eyes on Jeff at their wedding I knew one day I'd have him, so when he offered to take me horseback riding for a bit of sightseeing on my last day there, of course I said yes. My time was running out and I wasn't one to allow an opportunity to slip by, especially when I was feeling so horny after being with them for three whole weeks.

My cousin had to work and she obviously had no idea how I felt about Jeff, even insisting where he take me and what food to pack in the hamper. We waved her off and made our way to the stables to saddle up.

With my thighs spread across the horse's mighty back we galloped along. Jeff had packed a picnic hamper and with the saddle rubbing hard against my pussy I found I was beginning to feel another hunger grow – not for what was inside the hamper, but for what was in his trousers, namely his cock.

We spurred the horses through the sandy edges of an isolated beach, sea spray flying high to refresh me before climbing up a steep embankment. We came upon a secluded area enclosed by dense trees. Grass, thick with fallen leaves, provided a comfortable setting and the pungent aroma of earthiness, combined with the saltiness of the sea, had my senses reeling. The rawness of the environment definitely heightened my desire.

After spreading the blanket out onto the lush grass I lay down upon it and watched Jeff's broad back with an insatiable hunger as his muscles flexed while unpacking the food.

'Looks like you've packed too much,' I said, chewing on a blade of grass.

'You never know how hungry you can get when you're out riding,' he answered. 'Could get thrown from the horse, or it could gallop off and leave you stranded and alone. At least you'd have plenty of food to eat.'

'I'd just find the nearest neighbour, get them to take me back home,' I said smugly.

'But around here there aren't any neighbours. No one for miles around. You can scream until you're hoarse.' He chuckled over the pun on "horse". 'No one would ever hear you.'

'You mean we're all alone out here, totally isolated from the rest of the world?' I asked.

'Yep,' he said. 'Just you and me.'

'Well, at least I've got you to protect and feed me,' I pouted, as sexily as possible.

He eyed me, probably sussing out whether or not I was coming on to him and I was, believe me. I wanted him, wanted to feel his weight on me, wanted to straddle him like I'd done to the horse, feel him inside me. It took all my willpower not to make the first move.

Kneeling beside him, I allowed him to tease me with a strawberry. He placed the fruit just out of reach of my mouth, and as I attempted to bite into it, he pulled back. This went on for a while, so I lunged toward him, held his wrist tight with both hands, enjoying the feel of a tingle deep inside me as my lips grazed his thick fingers, before biting off some fruit.

Then I too grabbed a strawberry, teasing him as he had done to me, but instead of biting into it, he sucked my fingers, strawberry and all, into his mouth. The laughter died on my lips, only to be replaced by desire, as his tongue teased and licked my fingers seductively. Then, holding my hand steady, he looked deeply into my eyes before biting off a small piece, acting as though nothing untoward had just happened.

'Delicious,' he whispered.

I could feel a blush creeping up my neck as he lay back on the blanket, his eyes narrowing as he stared at me.

'Why don't you eat the rest?' he said.

Flustered, I popped it into my mouth, busying myself by unwrapping the cheeses, chicken, and cold meats that he'd packed and placing them with the fruits on a platter. Dry biscuits, a bottle of chilled Chardonnay, and our lunch was complete.

'To a memorable holiday,' he said, clinking my glass with his after he'd filled them.

'To fulfilling all I desired to accomplish,' I said, looking coyly up at him through my lashes.

'I'll certainly drink to that.' He smirked.

We ate in silence. I was nervous as he scrutinised me, unsure of what else I wanted to say and if I really wanted to make the first move. He was after all, my cousin's husband, but he was also very hot.

He lifted himself up on one arm and again, offered me a strawberry, a large juicy one that dripped down his wrist. As I tried to bite into it he crushed it against my mouth, the pulp smearing over my lips while the juices dribbled down my chin. Like a man dying of thirst, he lapped at my chin, licking off the juice and flesh. It was so erotic and when his tongue snaked its way into my mouth I lost total control.

My hands ran through his hair, over his strong back and

41

down over his arse while his hands pawed at me, crushing my breasts, tugging at my trouser band and plunging in between my open thighs.

Desperate and hungry for sex we tore at each other's clothes, discarding them in a flurry to litter haphazardly about us on the green grass. He smothered my breasts with wet kisses as I lay there, naked before him, my eyes swimming with passion, unable even to focus on the clear blue sky. I held my breath as his kisses moved down lower toward my navel, then over my mound, tickling my hairless pussy as his tongue darted about my slit.

He opened my legs and nuzzled in between them, murmuring his approval. I lay there, pussy throbbing, pulling at my nipples, caressing my own breasts while my knees crushed his head as I tightened my grip, unable to believe a man could make me come in seconds.

He lapped at my juices as they oozed down his chin and then he was devouring me, driving me wild. I arched my back, peaking again, my nipples jutting forward as I pulled them harder, stretching and rolling them between my fingers as though offering them to him while my breathing became more laboured, more ragged.

He crushed a handful of strawberries, over my breasts and abdomen, smearing me with the pulp. As the sweetness drifted up to envelop me, my nostrils flared as his hand reached up and he slipped some fruit into my open mouth. I sucked on his fingers greedily, grinding my pussy against him but he pulled back and inserted something inside me; definitely not his cock, not hard or big enough to be that.

His mouth was back, licking my flaps, as he pushed whatever it was in and out of my pussy. I lifted my head to see but he was nibbling on my clit. As much as I didn't want him to stop I wanted to see what he was doing, so I pulled him away by the hair, his cheeky eyes staring at me over my mound and then with a quick munch at my pussy he was climbing up my body. He lowered his head to me with the distinct fragrance of banana all over him.

When he kissed me, the bitten-off piece of banana entered my mouth and we mashed it together, each of us biting into the fruit, sharing it in amorous longing for each other. His hand went into the pile of fruit and he smeared my body with cantaloupe, watermelon, and kiwi fruit.

I pulled him hard into me, pressing my body and the fruit all over him. We rolled around the blanket, laughing as we licked at the squashed fruit. Then he pinned me to the ground, pulling my arms up, holding them with one hand, forcing my chest to thrust upward as my stomach sucked in and my breasts beckoned him to them.

His eyes stared hard into mine.

'Open your legs,' he commanded.

I did, lying there quivering under his scrutiny while his cock pressed firmly into the side of my thigh. He ran his fingers down the inside of my arm, the side of my body and then over my mound.

'Hairless,' he breathed into my ear. 'There's nothing better.'

Letting go of my arms his hand roamed over my slit before his fingers probed my outer lips, pulling them open so his fat finger could snuggle under the hood to where my clit was hiding, waiting, anticipating his touch.

Electrified with passion, I reached for his cock, marvelling at the thickness of his shaft as my hand stroked and admired him. Precome was oozing from the slit. I lowered my head, flickered out my tongue and very gently licked his fabulous knob, my tongue lapping at the edges before my mouth hovered over the top of it. I moaned as my pussy pulsated madly, anticipating what was to come – namely me.

He threw me back down on the ground and I pulled him between my open thighs, inching my pussy closer to him, squirming until his knob was probing me. I held my breath, desperate for his magnificent cock to fill me up.

With one quick thrust he was fully inside me, going further than any man has ever been. He began pumping rhythmically and I swooned beneath him, my juices smearing his cock, wetting it so it slipped in and out deliciously. I pressed my open palm to his chest, pushing him away from me so I could peer down and watch the slippery monster glide in and out of me, rubbing against my bulging clit, swollen and throbbing, causing another orgasm to build up in me again.

I bucked back into him, wrapping my legs around his torso, kicking him with my heels, spurring him on. With a clenched fist I punched into him, overwhelmed with carnal lust, desperate for a good fucking.

He grabbed at my breasts, crushing them as his mouth came down to bite on my nipple. I screamed out in the still air as he sucked it into his mouth, fucking me harder. The horses neighed, momentarily startled. I punched into his back, crazy for more, wanting him to go on and on. I crushed my other breast but he knocked my hand away, eagerly sucking this nipple while pinching at the other one.

Pressure was building up inside me and I screamed even louder.

'Fuck me hard, you bastard. Harder!' I demanded.

He rolled on his back, lifting me with him. Straddling him like this, I ground down into him as he thrust upward. Punching my fists into his chest, I slammed down onto his groin, impaling myself, like a woman possessed.

'I can't get enough of you,' I screamed.

'You fucking horny little bitch.' He laughed, driving himself up into me.

Then he slapped me hard on the arse, the suddenness of it inflaming me more.

'Off,' he demanded.

'No.' I laughed, anticipating – no, hoping another slap at my disobedience would be coming.

'I said off,' he insisted.

'What?' I said, shocked and disappointed that he'd call a stop to the proceedings.

He grabbed my hand and dragged me to his horse. Naked, he swung up onto the saddle and I had a quick glimpse of his hairy balls as he threw his leg over.

'Here,' he said, holding out his hand to me.

'What?' I muttered.

'Your hand, come on. I promised you a ride you'll never forget.' He chuckled.

He hoisted me up and in a moment I was mounted upon him. It was high up there on the horse, and in this position, with his cock jutting upward; I was speared to the hilt upon him. Then suddenly he kicked his horse and it galloped off. He manoeuvred the reins while I hung on to him. Up and down I bounced, his cock hitting inside me so hard I was sure my lungs would be bruised.

'This is madness,' I screamed.

He laughed, deep in his throat, and I fleetingly wondered if we really were alone up here. Imagine someone coming across us like this? Watching us as we galloped along. Just thinking about it was turning me on even more.

I wrapped my legs around his back, smothering his face in between my breasts as I held on to his head. He lifted me by the hips and as the horse galloped along he held me aloft so with each galloping step his cock was forced up harder into me. He bit down on a nipple and I screamed out, enjoying being naked and alone out here.

I was delirious, being fucked like never before. There's nothing in this world that can compare to it. It made for the most amazing sex. I was screaming as I came all over his cock and he roared with laughter as my juices oozed into his groin and over the saddle. Then he gripped me tightly, his fingers digging into my cheeks, as he came in torrents, filling me up as the horse slowly cantered back to the blanket and then stopped.

We slid off the saddle and fell onto the blanket and into

each other's arms. The earthy smells that surrounded us held us deep in their fragrance as we lay there, cocooned in this wonderful place while our breathing returned to normal. My breath caught in my throat, pleased when his hand began to roam over me and with renewed strength we were at it again.

Then I was up on all fours with him behind me, ramming into me, his fingers gripping my hips as he slammed back in. I pushed back eagerly, wanting every inch of his massive cock inside me as my head flung itself around like a ragdoll.

He pulled out of me and I whipped myself around to take his wet and slippery cock into my hungry mouth. I licked and sucked, saliva running down my chin, until I thought my mouth would split, the girth of his cock was so huge. Then I was begging, begging him to take me back on the horse and fuck me as we rode naked through the countryside.

'Back on all fours,' he demanded. 'I want to fuck your arse.'

'Not a chance in hell,' I said, 'with a monster like that. You'll split me in two.'

'On all fours,' he said again.

'You're joking.' I half laughed.

'Never been more serious.'

'It'll never fit,' I complained.

'It will.'

Seeing how serious he was I had to ask, 'You won't hurt me, will you?'

'No.'

Trusting him, I did as he asked. With my arse in the air he knelt down and gently licked at the cheeks. He did this for quite some time until I began to relax. Then his tongue slid down the crack of my arse, up and down, even slipping into my cunt a few time. It was heavenly.

I felt his fingers pull my cheeks slowly apart and still his tongue was rimming me, slathering me with saliva before a finger slipped in.

'Nice?' he asked.

'Yes,' I whispered.

He pushed in deeper, finger-fucking me.

'Oh God, yes,' I moaned. I'd had this done before and quite enjoyed it but no one had ever had their cock up there.

'You like it, don't you?' he chuckled.

'Oh yeah, especially when you do it like that,' I said.

One of his other fingers was grazing my snatch, slipping in between the folds so much so that I couldn't concentrate on what he was doing which was obviously what he'd intended.

The next thing I knew his thumbs were digging into my cheeks and his knob was probing my puckered hole. I clenched but he slapped my cheek hard.

'Relax,' he ordered.

I did but cheekily clenched again, pleased when I received another smack and then another. I pushed back a little and felt the knob slip in. I couldn't believe it would fit. I peered over my shoulder at him.

'I told you I wouldn't hurt you.' He smiled, as his hands gripped my hips and he slowly began to push his way in.

I must admit I tensed again, unable to believe it wouldn't hurt. But true to his word it didn't and I found myself pushing back harder, enjoying the sensation of my first time at arse fucking. Before long he was slamming into me and I can't explain it exactly, can't explain what it did to me but it made me have the most powerful of orgasms, so much so that my knees buckled and I almost collapsed on my arms from the sheer magnitude of it.

When he'd had his fill he gently pulled himself from me and cradled me in his arms.

'That was the best fuck I've ever had,' he said.

'Me too,' I whispered.

'You want to go back?'

'Not yet. How about another go on the horse? I loved

that,' I begged.

'Your wish is my command.'

And, like Prince Charming, he mounted the horse and then had me mount him, taking us down to the still secluded beach. With no one about we fucked as the horse galloped through the ocean, cold sprays of water causing me to squeal in delight.

Finally, three hours later, totally satisfied, we dressed and make our way home with no one the wiser.

I've promised to go back again, soon, very soon, and next time I do I'll be bringing back my movie camera. With a cock like Jeff's I'm sure I could spend hours keeping myself amused – but, more importantly, I want to be able to show all my friends back home exactly how well the studs are hung in New Zealand, and by that I don't mean the horses.

A Lesson Learned
by Kyoko Church

Things had been a little strained in Shirley's house lately.

Strained, ever since she and Marcus made their instant messaging discovery – she a little later than him. Their own Internet version of *The Piña Colada Song* resulted in feelings of betrayal and guilt in both of them, rendering their house silent, but with the unsaid words creating a tension, as if those silent words were present and hanging in the air between them.

Shirley realised now that she had felt suffocated by their hemmed-in lifestyle. Suffocated and unfulfilled. They both had been playing roles: she the good little wife; he the strong and stoic husband. They unconsciously made up mannequins of those roles, like empty shells they then tried to jam themselves into. They just didn't fit. And the effort and frustration of trying to make it fit had been driving them apart.

Now, though. Shirley thought she might gladly go back, gladly take unfulfilled over the churning in her stomach the tension in her marriage was creating. Finally she could stand it no longer. *They couldn't continue on this way*. She and Marcus needed to talk. But when she finally reached out to him, she used the medium that had served them so well, and yet had done all the damage in the first place.

She messaged Master G.

SexyShirley36: Sweetheart, can't we talk about this? I know I was wrong. But you were too. It seems we both want something more. There were parts of ourselves we were holding back. How long until we can be honest with each other?

Shirley waited. A while. It said he was online. But there was no response. And then.

Master G: When I'm horny and it's not Friday I masturbate while I think about fucking you.

Holy crap.
Marcus?
Shirley figured this wouldn't be a big admission for most men. But Marcus never talked about touching himself and she had certainly never seen him do it. So often she'd wanted to break free of their ho hum Friday night sex ritual, had wanted him more often, in different ways. Why hadn't he told her?
But before she could ask there was this:

Master G: Your turn.

Shirley's face turned bright red and her heart started racing in her chest. Her? What did she have to say? *You know what you have to say.*

Master G: You asked for this. You asked for honesty. Was it only supposed to come from me? R we going to do this?

Okay, Shirley thought. All right. Here goes. She took a breath. And then typed.

SexyShirley36: I want you to dominate me.

Master G: Good girl. Go on.

Shirley smiled slightly at Marcus resuming some of his old Master G style. Her domination admission made her heart feel like it was going to beat out of her chest but his "good girl" response injected a little bit of mischievous fun into the mix. Made her feel a little reckless. *What's there to lose? You want honesty. He wants honesty. So tell him.*

Suddenly a torrent of words poured from her fingers on to the keyboard.

SexyShirley36: What I mean is, I want you to tell me what a horny slut I am for being constantly wet from wanting you. And for touching myself and making myself come. I want you to explain to me that my body is yours, every part. I exist solely to provide pleasure to you. I want you to punish me, teach me a lesson for being so horny and impatient. You would teach me this lesson by stripping me, tying me up and teasing me unmercifully until I was begging for release. Then you would explain to me that my pussy is yours and you are the only one who is allowed to make it come. And that if you allow me to come it will only be for your amusement, not because I deserve release. Only because you enjoy watching me come.

Realising she'd been typing furiously with him waiting, she

pressed "enter" and then continued quickly, as if whatever demon, whatever courage, whatever whim had entered her mind and allowed her finally to release all of these pent up, secret desires might suddenly leave her, leave as quickly as it had come. And she didn't want to live another second without Marcus knowing the truth.

SexyShirley36: When we're alone, in bed, I want to serve you. I want to call you "sir". I want to be your sex slave. I want to always ask for permission to come and to only sometimes be allowed.

It was only at this point that Shirley stopped and realised she hadn't heard anything from Marcus in a while. She had felt free for a moment, as though she were typing to Master G. But what would Marcus think? Confused, she stopped, suddenly worried that Marcus was sitting at his computer appalled and disgusted. But wait, Marcus *was* Master G, she reminded herself.

Then came his response.

Master G: I won't let you come often. You're a wet little slutty pussy and u need to learn patience, so I will ration your orgasms. Your wanting and impatience amuses me. When I do let you come it will be slow. Maybe I'll use a feather or a paint brush, so the feelings are just enough to push you over the edge, to make your pussy contract. But not enough to satisfy your hungry pussy that I know only wants to clench around my hard cock.

My God.

Shirley pressed her legs together and felt herself throb in excitement. His words sent her head into a swimming mass of lust and confusion. Marcus? Master G? Somehow she couldn't meld the two personalities who had seemed so separate in her head into the one man she now logically knew he was. Did it really matter?

SexyShirley36: Do you want to know more? There is more ...

Master G: Tell me all of it

Their confessions went on for an hour. After an hour Marcus couldn't put off work any more and they signed off then. But the anticipation of her husband coming home that day left Shirley practically jumping out of her skin, beyond horny and desperately watching the clock, waiting for the sound of his key in the front door. When he finally did arrive he barely got the door closed behind him before Shirley was on him. He wordlessly pushed her to the ground, on her knees, unbuckled his trousers, took out his cock and pumped it in and out of her mouth, exploding in a matter of minutes. When he was finished Shirley only looked up at him, licked a drop of errant come from her lips and whispered, 'Thank you, sir.'

During their confessions that first day, the confessions that elicited the front door "greeting", Marcus admitted to his wife that, despite all his protestations to the contrary, he did in fact very much want her to go down on him and fantasised about it all the time.

Shirley, in turn, confessed that not only would she not mind going down on her husband, but that the thought of taking him in her mouth made her insides liquid with desire, her head woozy with lust.

'Slut,' Marcus addressed her in bed that night.

'Tomorrow you will write an essay. The subject will be how much you love to suck my cock.'

'Yes, sir,' Shirley replied, a small smile playing on her lips.

From: SexyShirley36
To: Master G
Subject: Your cock
I love to suck your gorgeous cock. You know this and you put up with it. You're trying to teach me that you love me to suck your cock but it's only for your pleasure and it should not make me so wet. You know that I will probably never learn this lesson but you are so patient with continuing to try and teach me. Sometimes while you're teasing me with your fingers, you stop suddenly and order me to go down and suck you. I go down and gaze at your amazing hardness. Just looking at it makes my mouth water as much as my pussy. I take it slowly into my mouth. I lick it all over. As I lick it I imagine how fucking good it would feel to have that wonderful hardness inside of me. I suck it all into my mouth and start to use my hand too. When I hear you groan, my pussy starts to clench rhythmically, as if it's calling out to your cock, fill me.

Their confessions birthed the most astounding new partnership. Not only was their sex life now everything that both of them ever wanted – exciting, daring, intimate, compelling – but their power play solidified their bond. The more Shirley gave Marcus, the more he claimed. The more he claimed the more she wanted to give. She was intoxicated by his passion for controlling her.

One night Marcus had been teasing her for over an hour. Longer than usual. Hard and fast. Slow and soft. Stop, start. Over and over. Shirley's pussy juices were everywhere. She was a quivering mass of jelly Marcus had strapped to the bed. All she could do was lie there helplessly and beg. 'Please, sir, please let me come.'

Marcus just chuckled, told her no, not yet, and continued on. Finally, he stopped.

He pulled his hand away. 'I will let you come today,' he said.

I get to come!

'If you are obedient for a change, if you can follow instructions for once and be a good little slut, then I will gently rub you until you come. I will sail you over the edge and softly land you on the other side.'

Marcus paused. 'But ...'

Uh oh.

'You have to follow instructions. I want to see you come. I want your eyes. But,' he sighed, 'I'm not in the mood to deal with any of your other bullshit today. You will lie there. You will keep your eyes open. You will look at me. You may breathe and you may blink but nothing more.'

Fuck.

'One little move, one little gasp, you close your eyes one second longer than a blink and you will be punished. I will rub you hard and fast. I will throw you hurtling over the edge and then I won't stop.'

Oh no. Not that. Anything but that.

'You will come hard and fast. Just like your horny little pussy wants. But then, for disobeying me, the clit torture will begin.' He smiled then, looking down at her terrified eyes, a slow smile, sinister. 'Oh yes, I know how sensitive your tiny clitty gets after you've come. Your punishment for disobedience will be me continuing to rub that sensitive little button. Maybe I'll lick it too. Mm, yes, I think I will. Then you can scream and beg all you want because it won't fucking matter.'

Oh God, no.

'Are you ready?'

No.

'Answer me.'

'Yes, sir.'

'Then let's begin.'

So their games continued. Shirley thought she was somehow setting the women's movement back half a century with how she acquiesced to Marcus's every command in bed, and she could care less. She couldn't help it. And really, it was what she wanted too. Marcus knew exactly what it did to her to be made to feel small, insignificant, used. To be his plaything. After years of mechanical marital fucking on a Friday night – 15 minutes of tweak this here, rub this there, insert tab A into slot B, pump; obligatory orgasm for the little wife, perfunctory orgasm for the husband, sleep – to then experience wild teasing, gasping, screaming, begging, being her husband's little come slut, down on her knees, satisfying his every carnal desire ... Well, it was her every horny, naughty, bad girl dream come true.

She was, however, unprepared for Marcus making a dream of his own come true.

It was Saturday night. Marcus had suggested spending the weekend at the Falls, getting a suite at the Hilton, dressing up, going out for dinner. A mini getaway. During dinner, beneath the tablecloth, he kept one hand settled between Shirley's legs, not rubbing, barely pressing, just enough so that she was aware of the heat from his hand, aware of its presence and the control it signified over her pussy, over her entire body. Every so often he leaned over and whispered something in her ear. To an outside observer they might look like a couple newly in love, the man breathing sweet nothings into his lover's ear. In actuality he was saying things like, 'Hearing you beg makes me so hard,' or, 'I plan to lick you until you are a hair away from coming, so, so close. And then I will thrust my cock in that tight little cunt and fuck you while I order you not to come.'

She barely ate.

But that was OK. Because, back in the room, Shirley's mouth was crammed full of Marcus's stiff shaft. She slurped greedily at this gift her master was giving her as he lay on the king-sized bed.

'Let's see if you are being a good little slut,' Marcus said, reaching down and lazily stroking soft circles around her pussy. After his dinnertime teasing Shirley felt like there was a lake between her legs. She considered apologising. But then Marcus stuck two fingers in her hole and her pussy clamped down on the digits hungrily.

Marcus didn't get mad. He chuckled. 'Silly, horny, dirty little slut. You're not even trying to learn your lesson, are you? You are so wet. You're thinking about fucking me, aren't you? Answer me.'

'Yes, sir.'

'Come up here.'

Marcus pulled her up to him and gently caressed her quivering body.

'It's time for some harsher punishment,' he whispered.

Marcus left her there in their bedroom high up over the Falls for a few minutes. Shirley heard him in the sitting room briefly on the phone. Then he came back, got out the restraining straps from his overnight bag and laid them on the bed. She wanted to know what was going on but she knew she could not ask.

'Little sluts who aren't learning their lessons need punishment.' He sighed, poured himself a drink and sat down in an armchair by the large picture window. 'I need to bring in reinforcement.'

His drink finished, Marcus got up and, just as he now

regularly found it necessary to do at home, tied Shirley firmly down to the bed. Outside the bedroom she heard the door to the hallway open and close. Her heart leapt.

'Ah, right on time,' Marcus said.

Marcus had tied Shirley spread-eagle so her pussy was wide open, vulnerable. She heard footsteps approaching the bedroom door, high heels clicking.

The door opened and a woman walked in, about 25. She was brunette, olive skinned, with almond shaped eyes, full breasts and a tiny waist. Gorgeous. Shirley was immediately jealous and humiliated. That same feeling of smallness. It made her so dizzyingly horny.

'Bitch,' said Marcus, 'this is Slut. You are here to help me teach Slut a lesson.' The brunette simply smiled. She removed her trench coat to reveal a sheer black camisole that barely covered her ass. She was wearing matching black panties but when she turned Shirley saw that they parted into two straps on either side of her firm ass cheeks, leaving her bottom and pussy accessible.

'Now,' Marcus began, standing beside the two of them on the bed, 'the lesson we are teaching Slut today is not to be so driven by her own orgasm. She's very horny, you see.' He smiled pityingly at Shirley and then turned back to his new minion, who appeared to be enjoying this information immensely. 'So, here's what I need you to do, Bitch. Go down between Slut's legs. Lick her until I tell you to stop.'

The brunette held open Shirley's labia firmly, stretching her so that her clitoris was completely exposed. When her wet tongue touched down on that hyper-sensitive tip for the first time, Shirley cried out with the intensity of the feelings that shot through her entire body. And as Bitch's tongue continued to move expertly around her swollen clit, Marcus whispered in her ear. 'Does it feel good, my naughty little whore? Bitch knows what she's doing, doesn't she?' He chuckled then, low and dangerous. 'Don't you come. Don't you dare. We're going to edge you ten times. Bitch will bring you to the edge of coming ten times, and if you're good and can follow instructions, maybe I'll fuck you when she's done.'

Shirley writhed and panted, pulling in vain at the restraints that kept her immobile on the bed and completely helpless. Marcus was right. The woman knew exactly how to tease and tempt her sensitive flesh with her fluttering tongue directly on her clitoris. Shirley was close after a minute.

'Sir,' she gasped. 'Sir, I'm going to come ...'

'Bitch, stop,' Marcus commanded, and the brunette withdrew her tongue.

Shirley's tensed body immediately slackened on the bed. But Marcus didn't give her long.

'Continue,' he directed, and the brunette's lapping restarted.

Shirley managed to cry out for mercy four times, and four times Marcus stopped the woman then mercilessly bade her continue on after mere moments, hardly allowing his wife any recovery time. Shirley's legs shook uncontrollably. Tears poured from her eyes as copiously as honey and saliva poured from her cunt. Until this point the brunette had been licking Shirley's clit with varying speeds and pressures, barely giving her enough time to adjust to one sensation before switching it up with something different. It made it very difficult for Shirley to concentrate on keeping her orgasm at bay. However, on this fifth edge, the woman added more.

Suddenly Shirley felt three of Bitch's slim fingers invade her hole. Her pussy contracted and was quivering around the welcome intrusion when the woman quickly tongued Shirley's clit hard, harder than she had been, then fastened her lips around the tiny nub and started sucking.

Shirley couldn't get the words out, couldn't get any words out. The orgasm that had been looming, that she had been fighting to keep back, suddenly sprang out, was wrung out of her by Bitch's talented mouth and fingers. Her hips shot up off the bed. She opened her mouth but no sound emitted. Then Bitch's sucking switched back to licking. She licked Shirley hard and fast and as she did Shirley took one great gasp, her body convulsed hard and her voice returned.

Her screams filled the room, wild, animal screams that came from some deep place she previously didn't know existed. Her body would have thrashed had she not been restrained. As it was, though – pinned to the bed with Bitch's head between her legs, continuing to lap at her quim as her orgasm stretched on impossibly long – she could only scream; scream and shake and come. Come harder than she had ever come in her life.

Afterward there were consequences for her inability to follow instructions.

Of course there were.

Now that Shirley had divulged all of her secrets to him, Marcus knew exactly how to craft his punishments, tailor them uniquely to his wife's weaknesses. For example, Marcus was aware that after coming from oral sex, his wife liked nothing more than to be taken in his arms, filled with his cock, and fucked soundly until she came again, this time with his hardness filling her entirely. And so, for her transgression, for her inability to follow his clearly stated instructions, he ordered Bitch to continue licking his wife's swollen, now painfully sensitive clit while he fucked her tormentor from behind.

Marcus listened to Shirley scream herself hoarse, watched her jealous and helpless eyes take in the sight of him buried deep inside Bitch's cunt. And when he came, all over the brunette's back and ass, he rasped out, 'Next time, Slut, you better try harder to follow instruction.'

Good Girl
by Clarice Clique

'Are you sure your husband won't mind?' Andrew's hands were resting on the small of my back, his fingers stretching down toward the curve of my buttocks.

'I told you that we have an open relationship.' I tilted my head for a kiss that didn't come.

'Am I being bad?'

'Very bad.'

His frown told me it was the wrong answer, but still he took my hand and led me up to his bedroom.

My heart beat fast; I tried not to think about anything outside the moment, nothing beyond each step I took up his narrow staircase toward his bed. But thoughts rushed through my mind, from the pleasant sensation of imagining the firmness of his arse, to the heavy considerations of how easily we fall into stereotypes, me the bored thirty-something housewife, him the charismatic silver fox professor, both of us searching each other hoping we would find our own youth and purpose.

His bedroom was filled up with an iron framed bed and a mirrored wardrobe; a few books were scattered across the floor. He dimmed the light, making us disappear into the shadows of the room. With another man I would have reached past him and turned the light up to its full glaring power. Even though I'd waited over a decade for this moment and wanted to savour every second with all my senses I didn't tell Andrew this. I stood silent and still until he told me what to do.

'Take your clothes off. Leave the stockings and heels on.'

I obeyed him, twisting my body into the sexual striptease I'd spent my adult life perfecting. He sat on the bed unbuttoning his shirt and tugging off his trousers. It was impossible to tell in the dark where his green-blue eyes were looking, but I performed for him as if I knew I had his full attention. Silhouetted against the landing light, every part of my body was shouting out "look at me, want me". I danced and I turned, every part of my body desperate for him. Look at my tits, look at my arse, look at my legs, look at my stomach, look at my lips, look at my hair, look at me and want me.

I'd had lovers who would have driven the length and breadth of the country for a minute of my time; I'd known men whose fantasies consisted of the time my nails once brushed against their hand. That was the past; now my heart had given all my power to this man sitting naked on the bed. My heart had given all my power to this man the moment I first met him. It was only now his wife had decided she wanted time to experiment with other lovers that he cared about the things I might do for him.

'Come here.'

Our clothes were strewn on the floor, hiding the books. I stepped carefully over them and stood in front of him. He placed his hands on my naked buttocks, his skin warm against mine, but he did not squeeze or caress me.

In the days when we were still passionate lovers, my husband liked me on all fours with my rear thrusting up in the air. He told me and showed me in a hundred different ways how much he adored my arse.

That was such a long time ago. From standing in a church declaring my eternal love, I'd journeyed to standing wearing nothing but stocking and heels in front of another man and feeling like a virgin. Questions flashed through my mind, stupid, horrible, insecure questions that should never be in any woman's mind: what should I do, what does he want me to do, will I be good enough, is he still attracted to me now he's seen me naked, does he actually prefer thinner women to curvy ones?

'Am I being bad?' His voice sounded tired.

'No,' I whispered, running my hand through his hair. 'No, you're good. Very good. I told you, my husband doesn't care about me having sex with other men.'

Do lots of half lies add up to a full lie at some point?

I moved my hand from his head down to the hard muscle of his legs, brushing across his thighs with my lightest touch, circling around and around, with each movement drawing closer to his centre, until my little fingers brushed against the hardness of his prick, then I let my hand stay still the way his hands were remaining on my buttocks.

'What do we do now?' I asked.

'I've never been unfaithful in all my years of marriage. I've had opportunities, plenty of opportunities, but I never took any of them.'

'I don't think it counts as being unfaithful when your wife has chosen to move out and go and live with another man.'

It might have been too harsh. My eyes were adjusting to the darkness but I couldn't read the expression on his face. I held my breath and waited for him to say the lines about it all being too soon and it all being a mistake and we should stop before we go any further.

'You could suck my cock.' He spoke slowly, the tiredness had vanished from his voice, his normal tones fully returned; deep, sensual tones that made me want to drop to my knees and beg to be his sex slave for the rest of my life.

And that is what I did. I dropped to my knees, looked up into the blackness that was his eyes and silently begged for him to claim me as his. Then I parted my lips and took the head of his cock on my tongue. He tasted fresh and clean, no hint of shower gel or sweat. I pushed my mouth further down on him, my tongue licking his delicate skin, searching for his essence. His hands were on the back of my head, tangled in my hair; he held me as I took his whole length in my mouth, our bodies merging into one desire.

His cock was long and thick. I tilted my head to stop myself gagging, I wanted to have him inside me for as long as I could. It was him who pulled me off, yanking on my hair in a way that made me gasp with the intoxicating mixture of pleasure and pain.

'Kiss my balls.'

I leant back into his groin, pressing my lips around the tight little spheres. They had the same fresh taste as his cock; the scent filling up the dark room was that of my own sex. The aroma of my body's longing fighting with, and easily overpowering, the jasmine perfume I'd applied in the last seconds before I knocked on his door.

'Use your teeth.'

I bit down lightly at first, little nibbles.

'Harder,' he commanded.

I obeyed immediately by pressing my teeth together and digging my nails into his skin and my reward was a loud moan.

'That's good, that's good.'

The waves of heat rushing through my body at touching this man were more intense than the sensation of full intercourse with other lovers.

'Let me see your tits,' he said.

I was reluctant to move away from the hardness of his cock but I did not feel I had the power to do anything but what he told me to. I stood up so my breasts were at his eye level. He grazed his hand against my hard nipples.

'You've got great tits.'

I shone amongst the shadows of his room as if he'd said I was the most beautiful woman in the world.

'On your knees again. I'm going to spunk over them. Would you like that?'

'Oh yes. Oh yes. Please.' I dropped to my previous position on the floor and cupped my breasts for him as he wanked in front of me.

His fingers moved up and down his full length in quick continuous strokes. I was jealous of his hand even as my breath caught in my throat at the intimacy of seeing him pleasure himself. It could have been a minute or an hour waiting and watching before his come jetted out over my curves and my neck and my chin. He collapsed back onto the bed amongst deep heavy sighs. I rubbed his spunk into my skin and over my lips, tasting him for the first time.

'You can go to the bathroom and clean yourself.'

I padded across the landing to the cool air of his bathroom. I turned the tap on but I didn't put any water on my skin, instead I looked at myself in the mirror with Andrew's come dripping down my face and chest and I thought I was the most beautiful woman in the world.

Andrew spunked over me two more times, then my mobile rang.

'Answer it,' he said.

'It'll be my husband.'

'Answer it.'

'Hey, babes,' I said.

'Hey, you,' my husband replied in his normal voice which was neither happy nor sad. 'Just checking whether you're coming home tonight.'

'You don't want to risk me disturbing you midway through a porn marathon?'

'That could be a tad annoying, not to say frustrating.'

I glanced at Andrew. He was staring at me with a sternness, as if I was all the sinning wives in the world, including his own. As I looked at him he turned away from me.

'I'll leave now and be back in about half an hour.'

'Still time for a nice wank, then.'

'Yeah, I guess, if you want.'

'Hey, you OK? You had a nice night talking about all those old books or whatever you've been up to?'

'Yes. Thanks, it's been fun. I'll be home soon.'

'Great. I love you.'

'Love you too.' I spoke quietly. The words were dust in my mouth.

I gathered my clothes up without saying anything. We didn't speak again until we were at the front door and he was holding it open for me.

'It's probably best you don't mention anything of this to your husband.'

'He won't mind.'

'I would rather you didn't. It'll be easier if you want to meet me again some other time.'

I nodded. There was a pain in my stomach that Andrew had so quickly seen how much I wanted him and how easy it was for him to manipulate me.

'It's been fun tonight. I'm afraid I was a selfish lover. But it was very enjoyable. And not just because you're a former student.' The last part was rushed out in a manner that made me think I might have an iota of power over him. But before I could think about that or respond I was out of his house and alone on the street.

When I arrived home I found my husband lying in bed wearing a He-Man T-shirt and matching boxer shorts. I leaned over and gave him my cheek to kiss, but he put his arm around my waist and pulled me closer.

'I've been waiting for you to get back.'

I smiled a weak smile. 'I'm a bit peckish after all the reading and talking. I might go and get something to eat, watch a bit of telly, you know.'

'Did you have a good time looking at all his old books,

the first editions or whatever it was you were getting excited about?'

I looked at my husband and I thought of a few hours ago when I was snuggled next to Andrew on his sofa as he read me Rochester's poems, smiling with more than a hint of triumph and wickedness when he pronounced the risqué words.

'Yeah, it was a good night. Nice to meet up with someone I can talk about literature with. So, I guess, I'll go and get that something to eat now.'

'You sure you don't want to come to bed with me? I missed you this evening.' He let go of me and pulled his T-shirt over his head then slipped his boxer shorts off.

My husband's sex drive didn't stretch to more than once every couple of months. There were times he'd made me feel like a sexual deviant for having stronger desires than him, but there was never any time I'd said no to him when he was in the mood.

'Maybe you're right. I'm not so hungry. I'll come to bed now.'

I undressed slowly, smoothing the creases out of my clothes before I hung them up. I got a nightie out and started to pull it over my head but my husband protested.

'No, I'd like you naked, if that's OK? I hope I can warm you up,' he said with a little giggle.

I put the nightie away again and climbed into bed next to him. He fondled my breasts and I wondered if he'd notice the dried come clinging to my skin.

'You've got great tits,' he said.

'Thank you.'

Something sunk heavy inside me. I was betraying the man I loved, the time I'd spent with him, by giving my body to my husband so soon after leaving Andrew. Thinking of Andrew, even feeling guilty about Andrew, sent a surge through my body as if I was kneeling in front of him right now, my breasts pressed around his cock, his moans filling

67

the air. My husband was moving to mount me, but I pushed his shoulders back and climbed on top of him, pinning him down with my weight. I closed my eyes and I wasn't grinding against my husband; I was back in the darkness of Andrew's bedroom, riding his cock hard. The sweat dripped down me, my back arched and I screamed out my passion.

When I opened my eyes I saw my husband below me, his eyes wide and his cheeks flushed. He looked unbelievably young.

'You should go and read your friend's books more often.' He smiled up at me and in the innocence of his face I couldn't tell whether he knew or not.

In that moment if he'd asked me outright I would have told him the truth, I would have let my agreement of silence with A to slip into nothing. I could have been an honest wife, if not a faithful one.

'I need to get up early for work tomorrow,' my husband said, patting my hips.

'Yes. Of course.'

The moment passed and we both rolled away from each other and fell asleep in our customary back to back position.

Every few months Andrew would respond to one of my emails or pick up the phone when I called and we'd meet up. It screwed me up inside that I was the one doing all the chasing: on nights when my husband was out I'd lie awake in the darkness, not moving, not sleeping, trying to imagine myself into a woman who could ignore her heart's desires and rediscover peace in fidelity. I could picture the good housewife, dusting, cleaning, baking, all the time smiling, never making any demands on her husband, merely accepting him whenever he wanted her. Then the picture moved to that perfect housewife lifting her skirt and revealing her naked sex to an older man sitting watching her with an unreadable expression on his face. And once I started thinking about Andrew I had no will to stop myself.

My mind filled with the things we'd done.

Me in a school uniform that could only be worn by a sexually mature woman, him lifting the pleats of my skirt up with a crop and inspecting my freshly shaven pussy.

A collar and leash around my neck, my feet forced into five-inch high heels, him leading me to a bowl in his kitchen to lap up a saucer of milk.

Hog-tied in his bedroom listening to his sensual tones travel up the stairs as he discussed his latest publication on sexual jealousy in Victorian texts with a few of his closest friends.

Pretending to be a nun with a disobedient hand creeping under my dress as he watched through a crack in the door, ready to punish me at any moment he chose.

What he called arse training, which involved bigger and bigger dildos being plunged into my behind and spanking that left my skin red raw every time I tried to writhe away from him. If I took the biggest dildo without too much protest he allowed me to suck his cock and spunked over my face.

Then fantasies infested my mind of what I wanted to happen with Andrew.

Both of us naked our bodies entwined, my legs wrapped around his waist, our orgasms pulsing through our bodies as one. 'I love you,' I call out, unable to restrain my emotions any longer. He pulls me against his chest, I hear his heartbeat and tears wet my cheeks.

'I love you too,' he says stroking my hair, 'I've always loved you. Leave your husband and marry me.'

On one of the nights my husband wasn't out, we were sitting watching trash on telly together when he turned to me.

'I was thinking today about our marriage.'

'Oh?' Totally non-committal, but alarm bells were blaring through my head.

'How we've lasted so long when our friends have split

69

up. It's because we accept each other how we are; we don't try to change each other, even the faults. And we're honest. You have your lovers, and you know how much pain that causes me, but ...'

'Causes you? Present tense? Last time we talked about it you said that you'd got used to the idea because you know I can't survive on your sex drive?'

He shrugged. 'We both know how it is, that isn't what I wanted to talk about. I wanted to tell you how much I appreciate your honesty, that other people sneak about and lie and make up pathetic excuses and I couldn't live with that for one day, but the bond between us is stronger. You've always been honest with me and I'm so grateful for that.'

My husband squeezed my hand. His skin was dry. I dared to look him directly in his eyes. With all our years of marriage and knowing each other, I didn't have any idea whether he was genuine, or whether he was testing me.

'I was thinking also that maybe it was time we thought about having children. I mean, we don't want to leave it too late, do we?' He squeezed my hand tighter.

'Yes. I guess so. I haven't really thought about it for a while.'

It didn't matter whether he was playing me or not. I'd made choices in my life a long time ago and I had to stick with them.

'Means you'll get more sex for once,' he said and we both laughed as if we really were happy.

Five weeks later Andrew rang me.

'I haven't heard from you for a while.' The phone emphasised the sensual notes of his voice.

'I've been busy.' I took a deep breath. 'I'll probably carry on being busy for a long time. My husband wants to try for children.'

'What do you want?'

There was a silence which I didn't have the energy to fill.

'I know what I want,' Andrew said. 'I want to see you. This Saturday.'

'No, I can't. I really can't. It's our wedding anniversary. We're having a party.'

'Then invite me to your party.'

I took another deep breath. 'You wouldn't want to come.'

'Invite me.'

I gave him all the details.

'Don't wear any underwear.'

The phone line went dead.

I thought it might have been a tease, but Andrew arrived at the party to celebrate my 15 years of happy marriage. He shook my husband's hand, gave me a dry kiss on the cheek and presented us both with a present wrapped in silver paper and a gold ribbon.

'Thank you,' my husband said.

Andrew nodded and then merged himself amongst my friends, charming them all and making my insides twist with jealousy and pride.

A few minutes before midnight, when everyone had drunk too much to notice me, I slipped outside and filled my lungs with the cold night air. Under the shroud of darkness I let a few tears escape and reached into my handbag for my secret packet of cigarettes. A strong, familiar hand gripped my wrist.

'You know what I think of smoking.' His sensual tones caressed my ears. I could imagine that it was just me and him in the world, that the party happening a few feet away didn't exist. 'I hope you've been more obedient in other ways.'

Andrew's hand moved up my arm and down my cleavage. He rested on the outside of my dress, squeezing my nipples through the thin material.

'Lift up your skirt.'

71

I obeyed him.

'Higher.'

The hand playing with my nipples pinched down hard and didn't release. With his other hand he began to lightly spank my naked sex.

'Your husband is a nice man. You've been a bad girl, a very bad girl to lie to him.'

He spanked my pussy harder.

'I would be good if I was yours.'

He pushed his fingers into my mouth, forcing me to taste my juices.

'My wife is moving back in tomorrow. We've agreed to try again. Don't look at me like that; if you were honest to yourself you always knew you and I had no future. Don't say anything, make your tongue busy with my cock.'

I dropped to my knees, letting the expensive dress my husband had chosen for me fall into the dirt. I unzipped his trousers and found his erection, thinking that this really would be the last time. It gave an extra painful sweetness to this thing I'd dreamed of happening since I was 18, tasting his freshness, being filled up with his passion. He gripped the back of my head and mouth-fucked me harder than he'd ever done before. My phone vibrated in my handbag. I was barely aware of it and didn't think Andrew would notice but he immediately stopped. He picked up my handbag, found my phone and handed it to me.

'Rub it against your clit.'

'It's my husband,' I said glancing at the call ID.

Andrew stared at me. By the light of the phone I saw the intensity of his eyes and my body melted into his desire. I pressed the phone against my wetness, moaning as I watched his hand wank up and down his cock.

The phone stopped and started again a few more times until Andrew ordered me to answer it.

'Hi, babes,' I said. 'I'm just getting a bit of fresh air. Why are you ringing me?'

Andrew pressed me against the rough brick wall. He pulled my dress up and parted my thighs.

My husband's voice was slurred and full of pauses as if he had to remember how to talk. 'I just needed to check. Your blonde cousin, the hot one, I've forgotten her name. She says you don't appreciate me and she wants to take me home. I just needed to check how our open relationship thing works with me sleeping with your cousin?'

'Tell Louise to fuck off. You're drunk. Lie down somewhere and I'll come get you in a minute.'

'OK, babes. Thanks. See you soon.'

Andrew's cock plunged into me. I dropped the phone to the ground and could do nothing but scream.

'Don't ring me, don't text me, don't email me, make no attempt to ever contact me again. Do you understand?'

I gasped out a yes as his spunk shot inside me.

'Good girl.' He gently stroked my hair and then walked away into the darkness.

I picked up my phone and my handbag, took a deep breath and then, with his hot come dripping down my trembling thighs, walked away in the opposite direction to find my husband.

Applied Literary Theory
by Orlando Zinn

One sweltering summer a decade or so ago, I signed up for a course in literary theory to fulfil a requirement for the master's degree I was pursuing in Italian literature. A measure of the popularity of my selection was that only two other students had enrolled in the course: Ian was a tall, muscular graduate student in Comparative Literature, and Enrico was a Johnny Depp lookalike from my own department. Instead of spending the summer in the shade of New York's parks or museums or, better yet, feasting our eyes on the parade of flesh at the Jersey beaches – 'Wall-to-wall tits and ass,' my friend Seth was fond of saying – the three of us had chosen to while away our time in a stuffy seminar room discussing various theoretical works that often seem like required reading for insomniacs. I wasn't happy with my decision, but I had little choice since I had already put off fulfilling the requirement for as long as possible; so I mentally prepared myself for lengthy afternoons of stiff boredom. In retrospect, I am happy to say that while 'stiff' was certainly an accurate prediction of the effect that summer would have on me, boredom never entered the picture.

My reversal of fortune began with the click-clack of high heels against the hallway floor on the first day of class. 'Good afternoon, gentlemen,' the professor said, sauntering into the seminar room. 'I am Professor Battiste. You may call me Nicole.'

Schwing! Nicole was a knockout by any standards and certainly the most ravishing woman to teach in the famed halls of my alma mater. Her face was classic Lauren Bacall, enhanced by trendy auburn hair, piercing hazel eyes, and luscious lips flawlessly painted in screaming scarlet. A leather skirt clung like cellophane to her hips, a satin blouse outlined erect nipples and unfettered breasts, and a pair of fishnet stockings graced her divinely-inspired legs.

With my jaw on the floor, I listened as Nicole explained that as she'd recently arrived from Paris and was unaccustomed to New York's muggy summers, she was moving class from the un-air-conditioned humanities building to her apartment three blocks away. Double schwing! My mind filled with images of Nicole's 'lessons' in the privacy of her apartment. From the looks on Ian's and Enrico's faces, their thoughts were spawning similar fantasies.

Alas, the first two weeks of class passed rather routinely: Nicole would throw out questions designed to elicit discussion of the day's readings, and we would respond as best we could given the difficult subject matter and the distracting presence of our sexy instructor. She was always patient with us, though, and after our two-hour sessions we had usually covered the planned amount of material. As time passed, however, I found it increasingly difficult to concentrate on the material, obsessed as I was with my teacher both in and out of class. To say that I undressed her with my eyes would be a criminal exercise in understatement. *Oh-la-la!* In my hot and bothered state I imagined doing just about everything possible to her luscious body: devouring her delicious pussy, fucking her pouting mouth, ploughing into that tight ass, spewing all over those righteous tits. I imagined threesomes, foursomes, and full-scale orgies with Nicole and me at their centre; I cranked one off fantasising about her before I went to sleep at night and again when I awoke in the morning. Yet as I played and replayed the delicious scenarios in my head, I could only be disappointed by the seemingly inseparable gulf between fantasy and reality, for Nicole's conduct toward us continued to be consummately professional.

One day during the third week of class, I got so carried away in my steamy daydreams that I completely lost track of the discussion. Nicole was wearing a green sleeveless blouse that clung lovingly to her breasts. I lingered over the images I was able to conjure up from that single stimulus: Nicole's sleek back arched at a steep angle down to the floor, her tits spilling out on either side; her beautiful ass high in the air, rocking back and forth as I slammed my rock-hard dick into her dripping cunt; her face, turned to one side, revealing eyes shut tight and teeth clenched in ecstasy; her thighs ...

'So that the surplus of textual signifiers eventually exhausts itself,' Enrico was concluding in typically inflated academic language.

'Hmmm,' Nicole mused, '*quel intéressant!* What do you sink about zat, Zack?' She looked at me in anticipation of a prompt reply.

I felt my face flush with embarrassment as I tried to bullshit my way through an answer pieced together from fragments of Enrico's comment. 'Well, um, when the layers of signification reach exhaustion in that manner, er, it often signals an excess of meaning which ...' At this point I was completely stymied, unable to continue as my highfalutin' discourse was relentlessly barraged and undermined by one particular image from my interrupted fantasy: Nicole's pussy, dripping with desire, as it beckoned to me from behind the little diamond formed by her ass and thighs. As I felt my cock straining to burst from the confines of my jeans, my face went even redder and my words were reduced to incomprehensible gibberish.

'Well?' Nicole asked, refusing to allow me to save face. I felt sick to my stomach, unable to go on. 'Iss zere some problem, Zack?'

I was overcome with a disconcerting mixture of confusion, intimidation, and raw lust. A momentary lapse of sanity, in which I lost all regard for my aspiring career in academia, is the only explanation I can offer for what followed.

'Yes,' I replied with sudden calm, 'there's a big problem. Huge, in fact.'

Seemingly taken aback by my enigmatic reply, Nicole could only respond with a raised eyebrow and a palm-upward gesture of the hand, as if to say, 'Well, let's hear it.'

Needing no further prompting, I immediately stood up and faced directly toward the chair in which she sat, about eight feet away. 'This is my problem,' I replied, unzipping my jeans to liberate my ferocious hard-on, which burst happily from its confines and pointed in accusatory fashion directly at the cause of its present excitement.

A dumbfounded silence filled the room. Ian looked on in horrified embarrassment. Enrico, while stunned by my virile display, seemed to be suppressing a complicit smile.

Nicole's reaction, however, caused me immediately to regret my foolishness. The initial shock on her face gave way to contempt and then to cold calculation, as if she were counting the ways she would bust my balls. I felt a cold sweat overtake me as I contemplated, in the span of a few seconds, the grim possibilities: a charge of sexual harassment, expulsion from graduate school, professional disqualification, ostracism by my peers ... My dick began to shrivel in retreat from the menacing glare that now confronted it.

And then the unthinkable happened. The contemptuous expression on Nicole's face gave way to one of mischievous intrigue, and her scornful frown was replaced by a faint but unmistakable smile. 'So,' she said, breaking the awkward silence, 'Ian and Enrico, do you 'ave ze same problem?' As she spoke, she slowly undid the top button of her blouse, revealing the upper reaches of her plunging cleavage.

As soon as my dazzled brain had registered the implications of Nicole's words and gestures, it sent a message down south to cease retreat, that victory was in sight. In pious obedience, my organ began to lurch back to attention. I couldn't believe it! My fantasies, which just seconds ago had seemed like the cause of my certain ruin, were now poised to come true. My classmates too were stunned but clearly delighted at the breathtaking turn of events. Ian had lost all traces of his horrified expression, and Enrico's faint smile had grown into an ear-to-ear grin. Together they leaped to their feet and in no time were proudly displaying their own excited members in reply to Nicole's question.

'Well, zere's only one sing to do about zis,' Nicole continued. With excruciating deliberation, she resumed the unbuttoning of her blouse and sauntered toward us, tits swaying as she moved. The second liberated button gave us our first full view of her cleavage; with the third she inhaled deeply, and the opening in her shirt widened just enough to reveal the outermost regions of her rosy nipples. The fourth button showed off her navel, and with the fifth she concluded part one of her striptease, exposing a pair of mammaries that would be any red-blooded boy's wet dream: round and firm, the perfect size for a wandering hand or aching cock. She threw down her blouse with a triumphant air and continued moving toward us. Our dicks needed no further convincing and honoured her approach with a fully armed, three-gun salute.

We quickly freed ourselves from the rest of our clothes, but Nicole kept her skirt on for the moment. Apparently what she craved first and foremost was a large mouthful of red meat. She dropped to her knees in anticipation, and we accommodated her wishes by forming a tight huddle around her. With a cock everywhere she turned, she began by lightly stroking them with the tips of her fingers; she strummed with the skill of a virtuoso and watched as our organs reacted by swaying clumsily back and forth. She then substituted her face for her fingers, fondling our throbbing members with her cheek, neck, and lips. We watched in delight as a glistening spider web of pre-ejaculate was traced across her face, and from delight we were plunged into ecstasy when she at last opened her mouth and applied her lips and tongue to our cocks with long, wet strokes.

Her technique became more and more frenzied as she continued. Now and then she would grab two of her playthings and rub them together as she licked them up and down and tried to stuff both into her mouth at once. When she tried for three at once I felt myself about to lose my load and, not wanting to bow out so quickly, pulled away and decided to concentrate my attention elsewhere. I knelt down in front of her and, while she continued to blow Ian and Enrico on either side of me, began to fondle her breasts. Squeezing one in each hand, I licked them up and down, tickling her nipples with my tongue and watching as they contracted and hardened. When my urge to come had subsided, I squeezed her tits together and thrust my cock in between.

After fucking her this way for a while, I shifted my attention to Nicole's shapely legs. She sat Indian-style as she sucked my classmates' dicks, giving me easy access up her skirt. I started by kissing and caressing her stocking-clad knees; the course feel of the material against my hands and lips was an immense turn on. As I worked my way up her thighs, I reached the point where the stockings ended and were held in place by two straps tethered to a garter belt. I briefly checked my advance at this point, savouring the contrast between the rough stockings and the soft, supple skin they covered. Resuming my sensual journey to the promised land, I discovered a pair of skimpy panties soaked through with Nicole's excited juices. I pulled with my index finger along the top hem and, inserting the rest of my hand, ran my fingers through her silky pubic hair. It felt as though she'd shaved it into some type of design, but before I could determine what it was, Nicole halted the advance of my hand with her own.

Standing up abruptly, she undid the buttons at the back of her skirt and, wiggling her hips from side to side, slid her way out of it. With deliberately measured movements that kept us in heated suspense, she proceeded to detach her garter hooks from the stockings so that she could remove her panties, which she took off with one easy motion and tossed onto the floor beside her blouse and skirt. She then removed the garter belt but left the stockings in place. Looking up, she stood before us in triumph, completely naked but for her fishnet hosiery and high heels.

Nicole in all her glory was a sight that would satisfy the strongest voyeuristic cravings. As I devoured her with my eyes, my sight inevitably came to rest on her lovely mons Veneris, and I now saw what I couldn't quite make out with my hands before: she had shaved her brunette pussy in the shape of a V, a road sign pointing to the tourist attraction below. Between the two lines that formed the V lay a tiny tattoo partially covered by the neatly trimmed hair. Moving closer allowed me to make it out: a pair of Warhol-style lips, tattooed at an angle roughly parallel to the right half of the V. Confronted by the grinning lips, I had to smile back and couldn't keep from reaching out to fondle Nicole's artistically rendered bush.

Clearly delighted by my behaviour, Nicole looked me straight in the eye and asked, 'You want to – 'ow do you say it – eat my pussy?' Spoken by a gorgeous naked woman in that to-die-for accent, the words could have worked more wonders than an overdose of Viagra, but I needed no convincing. There's nothing I'd rather do on a lazy summer afternoon than eat pussy, and I salivated in anticipation of burying my face in my teacher's luscious French cunt. I lay on the floor beneath her, told her to resume her skilful cocksucking, and pulled her by the hips squarely onto my face.

Maddened with desire for Nicole's vanilla-scented pussy, I began licking and sucking while I penetrated her with my right index and middle fingers. She writhed her hips, grinding her flesh into my face and covering me with her juices. I heard muffled moans from above and glanced up through her cleavage. From my worm's-eye perspective, her tits were mountains of jiggling flesh above which my classmates' rock-hard cocks jousted for the expert attention of their teacher as she moved her mouth back and forth between them. Soon Enrico was spewing all over her lovely face and into her open mouth. Not to be outdone, Ian promptly withdrew from Nicole's mouth and, using a hand to speed himself along, added his own ingredients to the homemade beauty mask. The sticky offering dripped down her chin and onto her chest, between her tits, and down her torso, where it worked its way through her pubic hair and mingled with the honey flowing from her cunt. I feasted on the sweet-and-sour mixture until Nicole's body had been racked by the tremors of successive orgasms.

At that point I was struck by the urge to fulfil the fantasy in which my daydream had absorbed me. Crawling out from beneath Nicole's legs, I ordered her on all fours, ass high in the air and chest against the floor. It was just like I'd imagined: her breasts flattened out on either side of her back while her pussy peered invitingly at me from behind her legs and ass. I began slamming into her with all my might, watching my cock appear and disappear into her flesh, feeling her vaginal muscles contract in pleasure. After observing this scene for a few minutes, Enrico and Ian became hard again and were soon nudging their dicks back toward Nicole's greedy mouth. Resting on her elbows, she again took one in each hand and sucked while being fucked from behind. Now and then the force of my thrusts would impel her forward a little too far and she would gag on whichever lucky cock happened to be in her mouth.

After a few minutes at this pace, Enrico blew his load for the second time and collapsed onto the couch, his dick lurching in post-orgasmic bliss. Ian and I took the opportunity to suggest to Nicole a variation in position. Eager to please, she moved to the dining room table, which was littered with the books we'd discussed that day. Sweeping them to one side, she hopped onto the table and lay on her back, legs spread like a butterfly, letting us decide the next move. Feeling a little orally neglected, I approached her from the top and positioned her so that her head hung over the end of the table. As I began fucking her mouth, Ian placed himself between her legs. My companion from Comparative Literature had the body of a Calvin Klein model and was hung like a horse, so it was a thrill to watch him hammer Nicole's pussy as she rested her stocking-clad legs on his shoulders. With so much sensory overload I soon reached my breaking point. I withdrew from Nicole's mouth and aimed my dick at her chest, whitewashing her tits as they jiggled from the force of Ian's thrusts.

Drenched in sweat and semen, Nicole sat up on her elbows to admire the monster slicing in and out of her. Still standing, I watched from above in fascination as my come trickled down the landscape of her body, forming a little river that followed the sticky path left by the previous deluge: down the mountainous tits, across the valley of the belly, into the forested area between her thighs. There it collected between the boundaries of the v-shaped mound and, mixing with the libations that Ian was soon adding to this erotic panorama, transformed the smiling tattoo into a salty lakebed. It was an image that quickly lodged itself in my memory and only intensified my already twisted fantasies about my sexy teacher.

The next time we arrived at her house, Nicole was sitting quietly in an easy chair, review the readings for that day.

This would have been a normal scene in any academic setting around the country except for one thing: the professor was completely naked. It was an immediate turn-on, and we prepared for another session of erotic pleasures. But Nicole had more surprises in store. I have to hand it to her: she was a true professional. She wasn't about to waste away her summer fucking her students – without teaching them something in the process, that is. And what a teacher! As we watched in awe, Nicole pranced around naked, asking us questions about the readings for the day and leading discussion just as she'd always done, but with the understanding that her body would be the reward for a successful study session. Occasionally, when we answered a question exceptionally well, we were allowed to fondle a tit here or a thigh there, but until we had sufficiently demonstrated our mastery of the material, we were bound by a strict no-pussy policy.

This became our routine for the rest of the summer session. Nicole always emphasized business before pleasure, but when the pleasure finally arrived, boy, it came in tidal waves! She loved giving blowjobs, and sometimes after studying we'd play a game in which we blindfolded her, bound her hands behind her back, and forced her to stumble around on her knees, mouth open and breasts heaving, until she came upon the nearest cock. When she found it she was allowed to suck it off, at which point she would scramble to find the next dick, with the same objective in mind, and so on, sucking and re-sucking all of us until we were too limp to continue. Other times she would play dominatrix, whipping us with her garter straps and forcing us to suck one another's dicks before being allowed a taste of her pussy. 'We are an equal opportunity institution,' she would remind us. Usually, though, she couldn't keep herself from the fun and, before class was over, was begging us to fill all her holes at once. This was my personal favourite: celebrating the end of the day by squeezing my teacher in a delicious sandwich, one of us ploughing her ass, another working her cunt, and the third fucking the taste out of her mouth.

One day toward the end of the course, as the four of us lay in a mound of exhausted flesh on the dining room table, recovering from our latest "study session", I noticed that our abundant ejaculate had spewed randomly onto one of the books that Nicole had pushed aside to make room for our ménage. I couldn't help but giggle: it was the work of a notorious French philosopher, widely read in literary circles and felicitously titled *Disseminations*.

Thus ended my initiation into literary theory, appropriately described in the registration materials as an "intensive" seminar. Indeed. With Nicole's fragrant, art-deco bush as my guide, I mastered large bodies of material in no time and even developed my own unique take on the different theoretical schools. Marxism: the exchange-value of pussy is understudied. Feminism: women are not objects, but it can be fun to fuck them. Psychoanalysis: fetishes are cool. Deconstruction: there is no outside-the-cunt. I learned it all, moving from sceptical student of theory to eager, er, practitioner. Even now, many years later, when I hear someone questioning the place of theory in the classroom, I can only grin as I recall my sexy instructor, her smiling tattoo, and her uniquely baptised copy of *Disseminations*.

Oh, Brother!
by Lucy Felthouse

I wasn't being entirely unselfish when I'd offered to give Marc a lift to his sister's housewarming party. His sister, Rebecca, was my best friend and she'd recently bought a place with her bloke, Paul. She'd asked me if I could help out with the move and, great friend that I am, I'd said yes. When I got to her old house to start packing boxes, I had the shock of my life.

Rebecca's younger brother, Marc, walked into the front room carrying something. That in itself wasn't shocking, of course, but I still felt my jaw gape unbecomingly. The last time I'd seen him he'd been about 11 years old. He'd also had a crush on me, which at 17 I'd found hilarious and gross all at once.

Now I found I was the one with the crush. At 19 years of age, Marc had grown up into an incredibly good-looking guy. Gorgeous, actually. He was wearing low slung jeans and a tight vest, which showed off his fit body to perfection. Rebecca had gone off to make some drinks, so I found myself having a good old gawp at his muscular biceps and broad shoulders as he bent to put his burden down.

I averted my eyes as he stood up and walked over to me, smiling. He bent to press a kiss on my cheek. 'Hi, Lara. How are you? I haven't seen you in *years!* You look great.'

'I'm good, thanks,' I said, a little flustered from his proximity, not to mention the compliment. 'How about you?

I can't believe how much you've changed. You were just a kid the last time I saw you.'

'And now I'm towering over you. Did you stop growing, or something?' He teased me good-naturedly, his blue eyes sparkling with mischief. I punched him on the arm.

'Shut it you. You're never too old for a slap.'

'Ooh, yes, please!'

The banter had continued all day, only wandering into flirt territory when Rebecca was out of earshot. It hadn't grown overly racy, but it was obvious there was something between us. I just didn't know how long we'd be able to ignore it.

Pulling up outside the flat Marc shared with some friends, I beeped the car's horn to announce my arrival. I flipped the sun visor down, quickly checking my reflection in its mirror. Seeing movement out of the corner of my eye, I quickly put the visor back up and looked over to see Marc walking up the driveway toward my car. At that moment I knew I was doomed.

He was wearing smart jeans and shoes, with a white shirt. His dark hair was in a fashionably messy style – the type that looked like no time at all had been spent doing it, but in reality it had probably taken him half an hour. He looked totally hot. Rebecca would not be pleased if she knew what I was thinking at that moment.

I looked straight ahead as he got into the car, trying to avoid staring at his crotch or arse. When he was safely seated, I turned to say hi and got a smacker on the lips for my trouble. Marc jumped back. 'S-sorry!' he said, his face reddening. 'I was aiming for your cheek, but you moved.'

Equally embarrassed, I brushed it off, trying not to make it a big deal. 'Don't worry. Belt up, then.' With that I put the car in gear, released the handbrake and set off toward Rebecca and Paul's new house.

Later that evening, I was trapped in a corner being talked at by some boorish lawyer type. Or he could have been an accountant: I'm not sure because I wasn't really listening. Sure, I was looking at him and nodding at what I thought was an appropriate moment. But my mind was elsewhere. On Marc, to be exact.

I glanced around nonchalantly and my heart lurched when a pair of blue eyes caught my attention. Marc was looking in my direction. I smiled and rolled my eyes at the lawyer/accountant. Marc smirked in response. I glanced back at my acquaintance; he'd hardly noticed that I wasn't giving him my full attention. He just liked the sound of his own voice. I looked back across the room; Marc pointed to the patio doors leading out into the garden. I nodded.

Making some excuse about needing the toilet, I walked away from the dullard. I don't think he even noticed I was gone. I scooted toward the doors, then passed through them into the garden.

A couple of patio heaters were set up, meaning smokers could come outside to appease their cravings without freezing their arses off. It wasn't too cold, being mid-May, but the heaters lit the area too. Not that it helped me any. I looked around and I couldn't see Marc anywhere. Then I heard a noise and squinted into the darkness beyond the decking area. I saw a movement and headed toward it.

Marc was skulking by the side of the house, where there was a space between the fence and the building. It was like an alleyway, but since it was fenced off at the front of the house, that clearly wasn't its purpose. It'd be full of garden junk in no time. But for now, it was our hiding place. Marc grabbed my hand and pulled me down to the end of the alley where nobody could see us.

'What are you doing?' I hissed, blinking as my eyes adjusted to the darkness.

'Rescuing you from the boring guy. What was he going on about, anyway?'

'You didn't rescue me. I rescued myself! And I've no idea; I wasn't listening to a word he said.'

'Well I found you somewhere to hide, didn't I? It's like hide and seek!'

'Yes,' I said dryly, 'except nobody is looking for us. It's just us.'

We were leaning against the house wall side by side, and I felt my body tingle as he moved closer to me.

'Just us,' he said, lips close to my ear. 'Is that a problem?'

'No, I guess not.'

He shuffled closer still, so our arms were touching. His fingers groped for mine, and I let him take my hand. My heart thumped in my chest. It was decision time. Could I really let this happen with my best friend's little brother?

'I always had a crush on you, you know.'

'I remember.'

'But I was just a kid then. I'm not any more, and I think there's something between us.'

I didn't respond. This guy had been 11 when I was 17. My best friend's little brother, for God's sake! Marc turned to face me, placing his hands on the wall either side of my head, forcing me to look at him.

'Tell me I'm wrong.'

'But Rebecca...'

'Fuck Rebecca. This is about us. Tell me you don't feel the same.'

Even in the gloom I could make out the longing in his expression. And though my lips wouldn't form the words, my body was screaming them. My nipples were like tiny pebbles and there was a delicious warmth between my legs that was getting increasingly difficult to ignore. I felt the same, all right. I wanted him.

My silence obviously spoke volumes. It hung between us and we maintained eye contact for several long seconds. The tension was palpable. Something was going to happen; it was just a matter of who would make the first move. By now, my pussy was aching to be touched and I was sure my underwear was soaked.

Marc acted first. Still bracing himself against the wall, he bent his head to mine and pressed a soft, closed-mouth kiss on my lips. He lingered, waiting for my reaction. Finally, my body overthrew my brain and I kissed him back, opening my lips to admit his tongue. I slipped my arms around his waist, grabbed his arse and pulled him to me. His hard cock pressed into my stomach, which sent a further jolt of lust to my hungry pussy.

Soon, I forgot about everything. I didn't know who I was, who he was; anything. All I knew was that I was totally hot for this guy and I wanted him to fuck me; now. I put my hands on his waist and pushed him around so his back was to the wall. I kicked his feet apart and stood between them. Following my lead, Marc slid down the wall so he was more my height. I pounced.

Crushing him against the wall, I moved in for another kiss. At the same time I slid my hands up under his shirt, moaning into his mouth as my fingers explored the delicious ridges of his abdomen. Moving further up, I swept my thumbs over his nipples which were erect and – judging from Marc's reaction – very sensitive. Pinching them lightly, I smiled as he groaned into my mouth. I ground my pussy against his crotch; getting more and more worked up as I thought about how it was going to feel inside me. The friction against my clit was amazing, but I wanted more.

I gave Marc's nipples a vicious twist. He grunted, grabbing me and slamming my back against the wall. He started to kiss my neck as his fingers moved to undo the buttons of my shirt. I arched my back, aching for him to touch my tits. He soon obliged, wrenching open my top and pulling down the cups of my bra to expose my breasts to the night air.

My teats puckered at the sudden rush of air, but Marc

was quickly on them. His hot, wet mouth enclosed one nipple as he brushed the flat of his hand across the other, teasing the already erect nub and making it grow harder still. I leaned my head back against the wall as he pleasured me with hand and mouth.

The feel of his tongue and lips against my sensitive skin was sublime. My cunt was so wet by this point that I was in serious danger of having a damp patch on my jeans. Trailing his mouth across my chest, Marc fastened on to the other nipple and slid his hand down to my fly. Popping open the button and pulling down the zip, he made enough room to slide his hand down, inside my knickers and to the wetness that lay within.

I gasped as his cool hand touched my fevered skin. Marc straightened up and leaned his forehead against mine as his fingers played in my soaked slit.

'God, you're wet,' he said, tracing tiny circles around my distended clit. 'I wanna fuck you so bad.'

I said nothing, parting my lips wantonly. He took the hint and drove his tongue into my mouth, kissing me hungrily as he slipped two digits inside my clenching hole. Groaning against his mouth, I writhed on his hand, wanting it deeper, faster. Marc obliged, roughly fingering my cunt as his tongue fucked my mouth. I was so frantic that I was bucking against him and when he used the hand in my pants to steady me against the wall, the pressure against my clit triggered my climax.

Marc pulled away and watched my face as I came, pussy greedily grabbing at his fingers and soaking them with my juices. His other hand was busily releasing his cock from the confines of his jeans and boxers. By the time I'd calmed down enough to form rational thought, he had his dick in his hand and was stroking it.

I grinned goofily at him, still high on endorphins. He smiled back, pulling his hand from my pants and sucking my juices off his fingers.

'Mmm,' he said, making my pussy flutter with need. 'That was so hot, Lara. I really need to fuck you now.'

'You got a condom?' I replied, mentally crossing my fingers and toes that he'd give the right answer. When he nodded, I sighed with relief and said, 'Then be my guest.'

As he retrieved his wallet from his pocket, I hurriedly kicked off a shoe and pulled my jeans off of one leg. It would have been much easier to have done it doggy style, but I wanted to see his face. I'm sure I looked quite the trollop, standing in an alleyway with my shirt undone, breasts hanging out of my bra and my jeans bunched around one ankle, but I didn't care.

All I cared about was the cock that was currently having a condom rolled on to it, and the person it belonged to. As Marc made sure the rubber was firmly in place, I unbuttoned his shirt, craving the feeling of skin against skin. Then I used the sides of the shirt to pull him toward me.

Surprised by my movement he crashed into me, crushing me tightly against the wall. My arse scraped against the rough brick, but I couldn't have cared less. Marc captured my lips in another toe-curler of a kiss as he reached a hand down to my jean-less thigh. Gripping it, he manoeuvred us so my leg rested over his arm, giving him easy access to my pussy.

Using his other hand to position the tip of his cock at my entrance, Marc pulled away from our kiss, only to watch my face once more. Then he thrust into me. My eyes widened and my hands clutched at his biceps as he stretched and filled me. My pussy clenched around his shaft, causing us both to moan at the sensation.

When he was in me to the hilt Marc paused momentarily, catching his breath. Then he began to fuck me in earnest. My cunt was so wet that squelching sounds filled the air. Coupled with the noise of skin against skin and the grunts and incoherent babble issuing from our lips, had anyone heard us there'd have been no mistaking what we were up

93

to. Luckily, we weren't disturbed.

The position Marc was in meant he was thrusting upward into me, and every movement made his pubic bone grind against my clit. Before long I was heading for my second orgasm, and I told him so.

'Well, I best catch up to you then, hadn't I?' Picking up his speed Marc made short, hard thrusts into my willing body. My arse was going to have some serious scratches on it by the time we were done, but at that moment all I could think about was the tingling feeling filtering throughout my body as I got closer to coming.

I was still clinging on to Marc's arms for dear life as he screwed me, enjoying the feel of the firm muscles beneath my fingertips as well as using them for leverage. But when I began to come, I dug my fingernails into his skin involuntarily, making him yell and hit his own peak.

I was a mass of physical sensation. My cunt went wild and I felt every twitch and leap of Marc's spurting cock deep inside me. My climax seemed to last forever, leaving me limp as I rode it out. Marc, sensing this, released my leg and held me around the waist as I came back to myself. Resting his chin on my head, he waited until my breathing had steadied a little, then planted a kiss on my hair before pulling out of me, using a hand to ensure the condom stayed where it was supposed to be.

'You all right?' he asked, snapping off the rubber and stuffing it into the wrapper it had come out of.

I nodded weakly, still feeling wrung out. 'Just a little wobbly, that's all.'

'In a good way, right?'

Smiling, I replied, 'Right.'

We got dressed in companionable silence. When we were decent, Marc crept to the garden end of the alley to see if the coast was clear. He disappeared momentarily and I heard a wheelie bin lid open and close. Then he popped his head around the corner and beckoned to me.

Amazingly, we got back into the party without anyone taking a second glance in our direction, or enquiring as to where we'd been. As we walked into the kitchen to grab drinks, Marc subtly brushed my back with his hand and whispered, 'Brick dust,' into my ear, making us both grin like idiots.

Once I realised Marc and I had got away it, I started to feel horny again. The memory of his mouth on my nipples and his cock plundering my pussy had made me all hot and bothered again. It seemed that one taste of my best friend's brother had left me hungry for more. I was so fucked.

'Are you OK?' Marc asked, looking concerned. 'You look a bit red.'

I moved closer, ensuring nobody could hear me.

'Wanna get outta here?' The tone of my voice left him in no doubt as to exactly what I was talking about.

We made our excuses and left, desperate to get our hands on one another again.

We'd promised to return the following morning to help with clean up. So after a night of flatmate-pissing-off sex, I had to dash home early to get showered and changed, then come and collect Marc again. Rebecca had eagle eyes; she'd notice if I turned up in yesterday's clothes.

By the time I returned, he'd sworn his flatmates to secrecy and we headed back to Rebecca and Paul's. I felt really awkward, sure that it would be obvious what had happened. As if our mad passion had branded us with incriminating "we had sex last night" writing on our foreheads or something.

Luckily, the morning passed without much incident. There was a hairy moment when Marc and I carried some bags to the wheelie bin and saw the condom wrapper staring up at us. We'd smirked at one another, then our eyes had flicked to the alleyway. Unable to control ourselves, we started to giggle.

Rebecca, ever the slave-driver, came out to see what was taking us so long and caught us red-faced and laughing in her garden. Without enquiring as to the cause of our mirth, she sighed and told us to stop messing around or there'd be no bacon sandwiches; our promised reward for helping clean up. Suitably chastised, we pulled it together and carried on helping, the occasional smirk and sidelong glances getting us through the rest of Operation Clean-up. It was the longest morning of my life. I was still buzzing with that I-had-amazing-sex feeling and I just wanted to finish so I could drag Marc back into bed. Needless to say, there was no more messing about. We ate our bacon sarnies and were out of there like lightning.

We haven't got round to telling Rebecca yet. We're both round at the house a lot, helping with gardening, decorating and the like. She thinks I pick Marc up because his place is en route to hers. If she actually knew that most weekends we just tumble out of bed and go round to hers, she probably wouldn't be so welcoming. Still, we'll cross that bridge when we come to it.

The Relapse
by Tabitha Rayne

'So you've missed the past two sessions, Jim.' Jim scanned the room taking in her books, her framed certificates, her legs, her thighs. She leaned forward and continued, 'We finished up last time with you feeling confident that you had your urges under control, do you remember, Jim?' Jim remembered all right. He remembered imagining the smoothness of her thighs against his four o'clock beard. He remembered looking everywhere but those thighs, trying not to notice the buttons of her blouse straining slightly when she breathed, threatening to burst open. He remembered mumbling an agreement to something; he could guess it would be about counting, breathing, relaxing until those pesky urges subsided.

'Good,' she had said. 'Good, see you next time.'

He had left and had gone straight to the bathroom to relieve the built-up tension. It was one of his favourite parts of the sessions; he saw it as his reward for being so good and not making an out-and-out pass at the very professional and very sexy therapist, Dr Gaynor Leigh.

'Jim, please, concentrate. Do you remember?' Jim caught her impatient glance and smiled. He tried to recall his "I've been a good boy" speech he'd been rehearsing on the way over on the tube but he was sure he could see her nipples harden through her blouse.

'Yes, well ... oh fuck it,' he declared and leaned back into the chair. 'I've met a girl – well, she's not a girl, and she's a horny little she-devil who likes to fuck just as much as I do.' There. He'd said it. He'd been a bad boy. It felt great. 'I met her on the train on the way home from here last time and we'd already fucked before my stop. She's a fucking animal.'

The doctor's face remained stony but when she spoke Jim swore he heard a certain huskiness that wasn't there before. After slowly and carefully writing something in her notes, Dr Leigh looked up.

'Do you think it would be helpful for you to tell me some of your experiences with this young lady?'

'If you think it would help.' Jim smiled with one half of his mouth and willed himself to stop short of winking. 'Well, the first thing she said to me after I'd sat her on my fat, hard cock was that she could probably give me the best blowjob I'd ever had. She had had plenty of practice she told me and was on a mission to "perfect her art", as she put it. I told her she should come back to my place and she hasn't left since.'

'So you had sex in the train.'

'Yes.'

'How did you make it known to each other that you wanted to do that?' She seemed genuinely curious to Jim; this was far more than the usual text book questions about how he felt – she wanted details and Jim was all too happy to oblige.

'I didn't have to declare any intentions as she already had her skirt hitched up to her hips with her fingers inside her soaked panties by the time I got into the carriage,' he said triumphantly, willing a flicker on Dr Leigh's face. When none came, he continued, 'She looked me straight in the eye, took out her fingers, licked them then slid them right back into her pussy again. I tell you, I was fucking rock hard and she knew it. She looked at my crotch and spread her legs further apart until she had to lift her foot onto the arm rest. I didn't need more invitation than that, I unzipped my flies and pulled out my cock which already had spunk on its tip.' Jim paused to gauge the doctor's reaction. Still her face was impassive but she had been jotting down more notes. He thought maybe he was overstepping the line.

'Shall I continue?' he asked. Dr Leigh merely nodded once while staring intently at the notebook on her lap. He wondered what he would have to say to get this woman outwardly flustered. For the first time since he'd begun his counselling sessions, Jim had no intention of staying on the sexual wagon. He'd had a taste of talking dirty today and decided he was on a new mission – to shock Dr Leigh, and maybe, if he was very lucky, watch her getting turned on by his stories. He closed his eyes and visualised the scene on the train when he'd first seen Selena, the woman he now realised was the woman of his dreams. The image was all too easy to bring to mind and he took a languid breath in and looked back up at the doctor.

'I stared straight into the woman's eyes as she stroked herself, purring, and watched her cheeks flush as she licked her lips and looked at my package through my jeans. I was in pain with the pressure of my bulge pressing into my zip. She motioned to me to stop in front of her and reached over with her free hand and pulled at my zipper. My cock sprang out like an Olympic sprinter out of the blocks and I could tell she certainly wasn't disappointed.' Jim smiled inwardly as he saw Dr Leigh's gaze drift to his waistband briefly before snapping back to her notes. 'I let her drink in the sight for a moment then I sat down next to her and put my hands under her arse cheeks and lifted her over my lap. "Wait," she said and although I hadn't heard her speak before, her voice sounded odd. She reached her fingers back up into her mouth and slowly pulled out a rolled-up rubber. She smiled and pushed it back and forth in and out of her lips and tongue with her two middle fingers. I remember me groaning and her smiling. She slid it right in to the back of her mouth and slowly pulled it out, showing me how deep she could take it. She reached down to the head of my cock and massaged it with the glistening sheath; it was soft and hot and felt like her tongue licking me, teasing me. While she unfurled it along my shaft she was rocking herself into my jeans and I could see her teeth were gritted in sheer desperation. As soon as I was ready, I lifted her arse and held her hovering over the tip of my cock. She groaned and hungrily jerked herself out of my grip and sank right down onto my dick. She was so hot and wet I could tell she was aching for it; she groaned and arched her back. Her tits were straining against her T-shirt and I pulled them out over the top. Her nipples were like tiny rockets between my fingers. I took her breasts in handfuls and tugged and rubbed in time with our fucking. She slid up and down my shaft. Her pussy was tight and slick and my cock swelled with come hurt; I'd never had anything like it. I reached back round to her arse cheeks and rocked her faster and faster. She was gone. Her tits, unleashed, bounced and danced in my face. I looked down to watch my dick slide in and out of her. She pulled her pussy lips apart to show me her hard red clit, crying out to be sucked on, but she was so hungry for my prick she wouldn't let go. She put the fingers she had been fucking herself with earlier into my mouth and let me wet them good for her then she reached down started rubbing her aching bud.

'Fuck, my balls were twitching, my cock was in sweet agony and as I felt her pussy engorge and release her hot come all over me. I shot my thick spunk right up her until I thought it would come out of her head. I came so hard. Then she said, "If you think that was good, you should try one of my blowjobs."'

All the while Doctor Leigh had listened, shifting in her seat every so often, making Jim delight in knowing that he was turning her on.

'Weren't you afraid someone might get on the train?' Her

eyes widened very slightly. He thought of her going over his story in her head again and again in bed that night, slipping her fingers beneath her silk nightie in between her cool Egyptian cotton sheets. It made him feel powerful and his cock began to stir.

'Of course!' Jim smiled. 'That was the biggest thrill.' Dr Leigh stared, her face as still as midnight, but Jim could feel the air where her thoughts flew, rushing and heating. 'The best part of the whole thing was watching our reflection in the tube windows. It was like something out of a film. Feeling and watching, feeling and watching.'

'But what about the stations? Didn't anyone get on?' The doctor was leaning forward ever so slightly, betraying her calm demeanour.

'Well, if they did, we certainly didn't notice!' Jim stretched back in his chair, letting his legs roll out to their full length, only a metre away from the doctor. As if catching herself, Dr Leigh stiffened and tucked her toes primly beneath her.

'Well, Jim.' Her eyes flitted to the clock above the door. 'We are running out of time today, but it appears to me that you seem to be having a bit of a relapse. I am recommending that we should up our sessions to twice a week until we get you through this little hiccup. Talk to Barbara at the desk; I'm quite sure we can fit you in again before the weekend.'

Jim gathered his coat and wallet from the side of his chair and made his way to the door.

'Thanks, Doctor Leigh, it's been a real comfort and relief talking to you today. I'll see you very soon.' And with that he left her still seated with her long legs firmly crossed.

Jim checked his watch; he still had a couple of hours left of work and reluctantly made his way back to the office. As the hands of the clock dripped slowly round, Jim fantasised about the two women in his life; Selena and Dr Leigh.

At last, five o'clock struck and Jim tore out of the building without even shutting down his computer. He had wanted to nip into his favourite little sex shop to get a gift for Selena but realised his train was due. It was only a half-hour wait for the next but the thought of a hot woman ripe for fucking waiting at home urged him on. He did up his jacket and left the building. Ever since his first encounter with Selena, train rides had never been the same. As soon as the doors swooshed and thudded shut behind him, Jim found himself reminiscing about that night. Now he had an added dimension to his steamy daydreams; the sultry Dr Leigh had obviously enjoyed his stories and the thought of his sex-crazed images flying around her mind made Jim rock solid. By the time the train reached his stop, it was all he could do not to break out in to a run to get home.

The house was unusually silent as he pushed open the front door. *Oh shit, she's gone out*, thought Jim, who sometimes worried that if he wasn't there to satisfy her immediately, she would disappear off somewhere else – to someone else for the relief she craved. It was with baited breath, his hard-on subsiding, that he checked the living room. It looked like someone had burgled the place; cushions were everywhere, there was a half-empty bottle of wine on the rug and everything that had been displayed on the mantelpiece was scattered over the fireplace and carpet. The TV was on with a paused DVD. Jim pressed play. The unmistakable sound of panting and climaxing filled the room through the surround sound. The lucky blonde bouncing up and down on the leading man's cock was obviously reaching the end of her part in the movie and doing it in style. Jim felt himself swelling again. *So this is what the randy little minx has been up to; getting herself worked up to pornos all afternoon.* He picked up a pair of her panties which had been carelessly flung over the back of the sofa and put them to his face. Fuck, she's been enjoying herself, he thought as he inhaled the damp fragrance. He paused with the fabric pressed to his face. There was something else; a perfume he didn't recognise but strangely felt familiar.

Jim had a feeling he knew what had happened and crept quietly through to the bedroom. He peered around the door and watched the scene for a second or two. Selena lay face down on the huge dishevelled bed. Her legs were spread open and the air was thick with sex musk. He silently took off his shoes and socks and undid his trousers. When he was naked, he crept to the bottom of the bed and clasped her ankles gently, pushing her legs even further apart until he had her arse and pussy in full view. They were glistening with moisture and he slid his hands slowly up to them. She stirred as he stroked his fingertips over her arse cheeks. He paused and waited until she calmed again. Slowly he traced the curve of her buttocks down into the crook between her legs where the wetness from her session alone began. His prick thickened when he thought of her getting herself into such a frenzy. She was still hot and sticky and his finger slipped easily into the crack of her pussy. She groaned in her sleep and arched her sex toward him. He buried his two fingers deeper into her and she wriggled on to them. She hadn't come already. She had fallen asleep trying. He smiled. *Couldn't get there without me, eh?* He kept fingering her but used his other hand to spread her cheeks and leaned in with his mouth. He licked his lips and then he slid his hot wet tongue from the base of her back down into her crack until he reached her fragrant arse and circled his tongue around the edges, then darted it in and out just a little while his fingers still twisted in and out of her pussy getting wetter and wetter. He drew them out and slowly tried to ease one into her bottom. He didn't want her to wake up yet so dipped it in just a little. She groaned and twisted and he paused, letting his own want grow until he had to put his hand down to his prick. It was throbbing and he knelt lower, making a fist around his cock, pumping it up and down

103

while he fingered her slowly.

Just then a long sigh came from up near the pillows. Jim twitched, senses alert. Everything suddenly felt a bit odd; he had never heard Selena make that sound before His eyes scanned the dips and folds of the duvets and cushions that filled their enormous bed. He froze as he watched a mound of bedding begin to stir. A sleepy mop of hair rose from beneath the pillows and a familiar voice purred, 'Hmmm, we were wondering when you'd get home ...'

'Dr Leigh?' Jim gasped with his finger still deep in his lover and his cock throbbing with new euphoria. He stared as she rose from the twisted pile of bedclothes like a Venus with her finger pressed to her lips.

'Shhh,' she whispered and crawled languidly off the bed toward him. She rolled her smooth, lean body up behind him and began kissing his shoulders and neck. 'Don't let me stop you,' she said and motioned to Selena.

Jim groaned in disbelief and joy as Dr Leigh reached up between his legs and started rubbing his balls and tickling the base of his shaft with her long nails. 'I said, go on,' she urged, and Jim slid his finger deeper into Selena's arse while his mouth watered for her cunt. He clutched her hips and rolled her on to her back. Her legs flopped open obediently and he pulled her lips apart. Her red hot bud was jumping out at him and he licked his way around it, teasing as she twisted her hips, trying to force his tongue on to it. Dr Leigh now had him in a bear hug, pumping his cock with both hands and grinding her pussy on his back. He could feel her heat and arousal all over him. He was desperate now and pushed his tongue deep into Selena, fucking her hard with his face. She woke up and grabbed his hair, pulling him into her, jerking and twisting. Dr Leigh slid off Jim's back and up to Selena, devouring her mouth with frenzied kisses. Jim lifted his face from Selena's beautiful cunt to watch the scene. The two women from his every fantasy were here on his bed in a passionate sexual embrace. Selena grabbed Dr

Leigh's hand and pulled it to her hungry pussy. Dr Leigh cupped her clit with her palm and slid her fingers deep into her while rubbing her bud with the heel of her hand. Selena started massaging and pulling at Dr Leigh's nipples and Jim couldn't sit back any more. He rolled his hand up the inside of the doctor's thigh and she spread herself wide for him. He pushed two fingers deep into her soaking juicy hole and she rode him desperately, bucking and humping. She was like a woman possessed. With one hand in Selena, the other grabbed at his head and he fell on to her pussy with his mouth. She tasted to sweet and musky – so like Selena and so different. It was all he could do not to start taking bites out of her delicious cunt. Noises and groans came from above him, making him harder and more desperate. He needed to fuck one of these women and soon.

He pumped his fingers deeper and harder into Dr Leigh and suckled her clit in time. She shrieked and moaned and ground herself onto him. He felt her hand working on Selena and recognised the noises of her mounting climax. Dr Leigh writhed and twitched a few more times before Jim felt the walls of her hole spasm around his fingers and her clit jumped in his mouth. Her hot rush of come gushed over him. He reached for the bedside table and found the little square packet already opened. They really had planned everything! He slid the rubber over his aching shaft and rolled it down as quickly as he could. He could hear himself panting and his fingers were trembling with urgency. He needed them now! When he was finally suited up, he knelt up and grasped Dr Leigh's hips, yanking her down the bed and up on to his cock. She straightened her legs up onto his chest and shoulders and he buried himself deep into her. It was so good, so wet, so hot, so ripe. Selena smiled lasciviously with the therapist's hand still inside her. He jerked his arse forward and fucked her hard. She shrieked and looked into his eyes with her bottom lip between her teeth. After a few more thrusts, Dr Leigh rolled him on to his back and took him inside her again. He stared at her bouncing breasts as she ground her hips and rode him ferociously.

Just when he thought it couldn't get any better than this, Selena crawled up the bed and crouched over his face with her glistening raw pussy just a breath away. He let out a deep groan of pleasure and sank his tongue and fingers into the hot pussy above him. Dr Leigh thrust hard at his cock and held his balls in one hand. He felt Selena twitch and buck in his mouth and he lapped and sucked with abandon while his cock surged and danced inside the therapist's expert hole. Selena came hard over his face and he couldn't hold back any longer. His come rose deep from the base of him and exploded into the depths of Dr Leigh. The three of them collapsed on each other in a haze of sex musk and panting.

'What the hell just happened?' asked Jim when his heart rate normalised and he had finally convinced himself that it hadn't been a dream.

'Spot check,' Dr Leigh said, sitting up and beginning to pull on her stockings.

'What do you mean, "spot check"?' He looked from one woman to the other. Selena just smiled.

'Well, when one of my girls gets a report like the one you gave Selena today, I have to make sure it's true.'

'What the ...?' Jim began but the reality of the situation started to filter through. 'You mean, the train, that night ...' He looked to Selena. 'It wasn't an accident?'

'No, Jim.' Dr Leigh was now fixing her hair and smoothing down her skirt. 'It's my own particular brand of sex therapy. I match highly sexed partners and monitor them closely.' She smiled and cocked her head at the couple she had just bedded. 'After all, who really wants abstinence?'

And with that, the startling Dr Gaynor Leigh left.

Cowgirl Honeymoon
by Tamsin Flowers

It was the fourth day of my fantastic honeymoon and I woke up as horny as a bitch on heat. I breathed in deeply to catch the intoxicating smell of my new husband and let a sigh escape my hungry lips. I slid across the bed to where he lay, naked and still in the depths of slumber, and traced the downy line of dark hair that swept down from his belly with my fingers …

It had been my idea to come on a ranch holiday for our honeymoon; I'd dreamt of being a cowgirl since I was a little girl and the smell of horses and leather always turns me on to an extraordinary degree. Kyle had laughed when I suggested it but when I'd said I was serious, he'd shaken his head.

'No way, sugar. You'll never get me up on the back of a horse.'

He was adamant but I'd wheedled and whined for months in to the run-up to our wedding and finally he'd relented. We'd have five days on a ranch and then ten days on the beach. He was so in love with me that he'd agree to anything, so here we were at the Cougar Brook Ranch in Wyoming, staying in our own secluded log cabin deep in the woods. For the first couple of days I rode the horses and he rode me. I was in heaven – what girl wouldn't be, with a hot stallion between her thighs day and night? Then, on the third day I managed to get him into the saddle. It hadn't gone well. He hadn't wanted to enjoy it and he didn't stop moaning as we rode up a hilly track for the view from the top. And of course, when he fell off, he thought all his complaining had been justified and he limped back down to camp on foot, leaving me to deal with the horses. Last night had been the first night since the wedding that he hadn't wanted to screw me stupid.

Kyle grunted in his sleep. My hand had slipped down to his swollen cock. It was certainly awake, even if he wasn't. As it became harder, it pushed up into my grasp and I squeezed it playfully. It was big and beautiful and it was making my mouth water. I moved in closer and bent over him, gently running the tip of my tongue from the base up the shaft to the pulsating head. Kyle groaned. He was definitely awake now.

'Oh baby, work your magic,' he muttered.

I took his rock-hard piece deep into my mouth and started working on it with my teeth, my lips, and my tongue. I knew just how he liked it and his hips started to grind in response. His groaning became louder and more intense; he was shouting out as I sucked harder and harder.

Suddenly I felt his hands on either side of my head and he was pushing me away. I looked up, puzzled. He'd never asked me to stop before.

'What's the matter?'

'You gotta stop, sugar. I can't go on.'

'Babe, what's wrong?'

'I'm in agony. I can't move my hips. My ass is on fire. My back is killing me.'

I burst out laughing.

'You're saddle sore from yesterday!'

'That fucking horse. He bucked me off.'

'Well, if you hadn't yanked so hard on the reins ...' I muttered under my breath.

He pushed me to one side and pulled the sheet over his rapidly shrinking cock.

'I can't do it, darling. The pain's too much.'

I tried to hide my disappointment.

'I'll give you a massage,' I said.

'No, no. I've just got to lie here and wait for it to pass. I'm sorry.'

I sighed. The fires were stilling burning inside me and Kyle wasn't in any position to put them out. I got up from the bed and walked across to the window. The view of the mountains that surrounded us was spectacular and the sun was already high in the azure sky.

I wondered how bad it was or whether he was trying to punish me for getting my own way.

'Listen, sugar, I'm sorry to have ruined your last day on the ranch. But why don't you get everything packed, ready for an early start tomorrow morning? I'm sure I'll be fine by then.'

'On my last day? Are you kidding? I wanted to ride up to Autumn Ridge today.'

'Fine,' said Kyle. 'You go off and enjoy yourself. Don't worry about me.'

'But you'll be OK,' I said. 'A bit of bed rest and then I'll come and play doctors and nurses with you this evening.'

I leaned down to kiss him but he rolled away across the bed with his back to me and pretended to be going to sleep.

I stomped noisily to the bathroom and took a shower. If he was going to be like that, I'd be better off riding with one of the wranglers who worked on the ranch. He only had himself to blame, I thought as I roughly towelled myself dry. Then I pulled on my jeans, a plaid shirt and my boots and headed for the door.

An hour later I was perched on the back of a piebald Appaloosa called Mohawk, riding out of the ranch behind the quietly spoken wrangler who'd been assigned to look after me for the day. All I'd learned from our brief conversation before mounting up was that his name was Tex and that the enormous black stallion he rode was called Jet. It was hard to judge his age; his hair was bleached light blond by the sun and his skin was tanned and weathered – a real outdoors man. There were plenty of wrinkles round his sharp sapphire eyes from squinting into the sun but his body was toned and muscular and he mounted his horse in a single lithe move. I guessed he was in his early thirties and he looked much fitter than my younger, sports mad husband.

I'd asked him to take me up to Autumn Ridge and as he rode ahead he didn't bother with casual small talk. The strong and silent type. But I didn't mind. I rode quietly behind him, thinking out the details of what I was going to do to Kyle when I got back later on. That's the great thing about arguing with a lover – the making up afterwards. Mohawk's rolling gate tilted my hips backward and forward in the soft brown saddle and without realising it I was gently pressing my pussy against the hard leather pommel that rose up between my legs. It was meant for holding on to but as a warm sensation started to rise unmistakeably up my body I quickly guessed that the cowgirls found another use for it.

As we rode on through the dappled shade of a grove of aspen trees, I tried to keep my breathing under control so Tex wouldn't realise what was going on behind him. I had to be careful as he would glance back from time to time to check that I was still there and I didn't want him to catch me in the throes of silently pleasuring myself.

I took the reins in one hand and let the other one slide between my legs. I was thinking of how Kyle had taken me from behind on our wedding night with a passion so intense that we'd broken the treasured four-poster bed in the little country hotel we'd sneaked away to after the wedding. Through the thin fabric of my tight jeans I could feel the burning heat of my aching pussy and I was desperate to feel Kyle inside me once again.

Suddenly Mohawk stumbled and pitched sideways. My concentration had lapsed and before I knew it I slid out of the saddle and fell unceremoniously on to the stony ground. The breath was knocked out of me and for a few moments everything was confused blur of horses' legs, tree trunks and stones as I fought to get some air into my lungs. Seconds later Tex was at my side, then kneeling behind me and propping up my head on his bent leg.

'Just breathe slowly,' he said in his deep western drawl. 'You're gonna be OK in a minute.'

He stroked an auburn curl out of my face and then lifted up one of my limp hands.

'You got a nasty cut here,' he said and I realised that I had indeed gashed my hand as I fell. I closed my eyes. I didn't want to see the blood; it would make me feel even dizzier. I breathed deeply and things started gradually to return to normal. Tex sat me up and I could smell his musky scent as my head leaned back against his chest. I remembered what I'd been thinking about before the tumble but this time it was Tex who was pinning me to the edge of the imaginary bed. Shocked at myself, I sat up properly so I was no longer leaning against him.

'You OK?' he said, climbing to his feet. 'I just gotta take a look at old Mohawk here.'

I nodded, not ready to speak, and watched as he went over to where my horse stood, favouring one leg as he grazed the meadow grass beneath the trees. Although Tex had the same bow-legged walk as all of the cowboys, he carried himself in a way that told me he would be red hot between the sheets. I'd felt the hard muscle of his chest and the soft caress of his hands as he bandaged my cut. The fact that I was now breathing heavily had nothing to do with my fall. I had to face the fact. I wanted Tex and I wanted him badly – it was the first time I'd looked at another man since I'd met Kyle nearly two years ago.

I got gingerly to my feet and leaned against a tree. Tex was murmuring into Mohawk's ear and then he gently picked up the horse's leg and examined the hoof. He put it

111

down and gave the beast a reassuring stroke along the flank; I wished desperately that it was my rump he was stroking like that and I had to bite my lip to control my ragged breathing. My heart was thumping in my chest as he came back toward me.

'Yup, he's lame all right,' said Tex. 'You'll have to come up on Jet with me. Mohawk won't be able to carry your weight.'

He tied Mohawk's reins to the back of Jet's saddle so the lame horse could follow us home. Then he gave me a leg up on to his own horse with an easy grin. I felt his eyes raking down my body as I swung my leg over and wriggled forward on the saddle to make room. Seconds later he was sitting snugly behind me, with the reins in his left hand and his right hand resting on his hip.

'Giddy up, Jet,' he said and I felt his thighs tightening against the horse's side.

I sat bolt upright, hardly daring to breathe and certainly not relaxing into the rhythm of Jet's stride. Although I was hardly touching him, I could feel the warm proximity of Tex's skin, despite the cotton of our checked shirts and the narrow space between us. It was at least a two-hour ride back to the ranch and I was already starting to feel turned on. How the hell was I going to survive the trek without making my feelings obvious?

But as I looked around, I realised we weren't going back the way we'd come.

'Where are we going?' I asked, swivelling in the saddle to look up at his chiselled features.

'Seeing as how old Mohawk is OK without a rider, I thought we'd carry on up to the Ridge,' he said. 'That OK with you?'

I swallowed.

'Sure,' I nodded, turning back to face forward.

But as we rode on in silence, I was finding it harder and harder to concentrate on the scenery. My back started aching

112

from sitting so rigidly straight and the low, rhythmic sound of Tex breathing so close to my ear was driving me wild. I wriggled to try and get comfortable and my shoulder blades brushed up against his chest. That one move lit the fuse and, defeated, I slumped back against him and gave in to what I now knew to be inevitable.

'That's better, honey,' he whispered.

And as he adjusted his position in the saddle I could feel the burgeoning bulge in his groin pressing up against the small of my back, while my mons was rubbing up against the pommel with each swaying step. My breathing became faster and, completely without volition, I knew my hips were grinding back and forth against his.

His right hand snaked up my side and then popped open the front of my shirt. I wasn't wearing a bra and Tex growled with pleasure as his hand encountered my nipples, already proud and erect as they became engorged with longing. He twisted and pulled them between his finger and thumb until I cried out with the exquisite pain, then he leaned me sideways so he could bend his head around to kiss them. A pulsating electric current ran from my breasts to the pleasure centre between my legs and I writhed against him, moaning uncontrollably as he flicked his tongue against my nipples and gently teased them with his teeth.

As I begged for satisfaction, he dropped the reins across Jet's neck and used his other hand to start undoing the buttons of my jeans.

'Feels like you need this pretty bad,' he said as he slid his hand down into my panties.

I gasped. Within seconds his fingers had found my clit but then they searched further round, stretching deep into the warm, wet recess of my vagina. I quivered as his experienced hand explored and sought out my G-spot, applying gentle pressure with small circular movements. Then, with his thumb, he started to stimulate my clit at the same time. He had me slung across his lap and was literally

113

playing me like an instrument – the sensations soared through me like music, building in a spectacular crescendo as I responded to his skilful touch.

As he worked his hand faster my pussy was awash with juices and flooded with pleasure. My back arched and my hips bucked as the orgasm ripped through me and I shuddered as he kept the waves crashing over me for what seemed like an eternity. It was like nothing I'd ever experienced with Kyle or with any other man. My soft moans had risen to cries of ecstasy and I was left panting and breathless. Holding me tight, he gently withdrew his fingers from my throbbing vagina and my body slumped against him like a limp rag. I was drenched with sweat and I could smell the earthy scent of my juices on his hand as he held my chin steady and bent to kiss me.

His tongue forced my lips apart and explored my mouth hungrily, and without breaking away from me, he slipped gently off the now stationary horse and pulled me down into his arms. I kissed him back; the monumental orgasm had hardly dulled my hunger and I could feel through his bulging jeans that Tex needed the sort of satisfaction that only I could give. I rubbed my hand over his crotch, pressing hard, and he responded with a low, throaty growl.

The ground was soft and moss-covered and we dropped to our knees in a small clearing of dappled shade. Tex ripped away my shirt and then his own while I battled with the huge brass buckle of his belt. As I got it undone, he pulled down my jeans and seconds later I lay spread-eagled before him in just my pale pink silk panties. He kicked off his cowboy boots and his jeans while I looked up, licking my lips and fondling my tits as I appreciated his spectacular physique. His rich, deep tan covered muscles that were sculpted to perfection but most breathtaking of all was the splendid cock that now stood free and proud, poised for action, above me. The skin was paler than the rest of him but dark veins throbbed along its astounding length and breadth.

It was like a giant alabaster sculpture and I couldn't wait to feel it inside me. My pussy was aching for it and my hips angled upward as I splayed my legs, ready to receive my prize.

But Tex wasn't going to be hurried. He knelt in front of me and grasped the top of my panties with his strong hands. With a yank they were off and I saw his eyes light up as he tossed them away into the bushes. Then his head ducked down and the next thing I felt was the tip of his tongue gently exploring the soft territory between my thighs. With long sweeping strokes it massaged first the outer, then the inner lips of my vagina. It flicked softly in and out of the dark crevice and then I felt his whole mouth latch on to my clit as his tongue worked around it in small darting circles.

My back arched as waves of pleasure swept through me and then I added to Tex's efforts by putting my idle fingers to work on my nipples. I twisted them and pinched them until they were on fire and Tex's hands slid round to grasp my buttocks just as tightly, adding yet another level to the sensations coursing through my body. But I knew there was a part of Tex that needed attending to and I couldn't bear it a moment longer.

I put a hand on his shoulder and pushed him back until he was lying on the ground. Then with a quick twist I straddled him in the perfect sixty-nine position. His fantastic cock was now staring me in the face and I didn't waste a moment. I licked my lips and gave his throbbing head the tiniest of kisses. It jolted as if an electric current had been passed through it, and at the same time I felt Tex's tongue darting into my fanny, this time from a different angle. Then I opened my mouth, relaxed my jaw and took the whole enormous organ into my mouth. I started slowly moving up and down, using my tongue and my teeth to stimulate his shaft, while with my hand I squeezed his rock-hard balls until he moaned. It was as if we had created a circle of current that surged through our two naked bodies while we pleasured each other in the deserted clearing.

There was definitely some sort of primal sexual connection between us because at the very same moment we both chose to change position. It was time for the main event. I lay back on the moss, my hair a sweaty tangle around my shoulders and my body already flushed with arousal. My legs were slack and spread wide and I pushed my hips up to meet Tex as he powered down into me. His cock was far larger and far longer than I'd ever experienced and I could feel it deep inside me, pushing further and further as I arched my back toward him. He ploughed his way into me with deep, hard strokes and I wrapped my legs around his waist, pulling his body tightly against my own. His mouth dropped first to my right breast, then my left; the nipples were engorged and he sucked on them hard as they stood proudly to attention. Every thought left my mind as I surrendered to his complete control of my body and the sensations that seemed to be almost tearing me apart.

His thrusts became faster and faster and he pushed up on his arms, arching his own back so he could plunge deeper and deeper. As I reached an all-consuming orgasm, the muscles of my vagina contracted rhythmically and I could feel the hot fire of his come inside me. We both cried out as our bodies shook and shuddered with our own personal earthquake. Then he slumped down on top of me and kissed my neck so gently that I shivered with delight. His cock was still inside me but I could feel it softening as we both lay panting and glistening with sweat and juices.

The sun was sinking in the sky as we slowly got dressed in satisfied silence. Tex rounded up the two horses from where they'd been grazing, while I retrieved my panties from the bushes and tried to straighten my hair.

'You sure as hell know how to ride, cowgirl,' he said with a grin, as he helped me up on to Jet's saddle.

We never made it to Autumn Ridge but I was still able to tell Kyle it was a spectacular ride when I got back to our cabin. I know I should have felt guilty, and I suppose I did, a little bit. But he had been acting like a spoilt brat …

He was still lying on the bed but he looked a bit chirpier than when I'd left him in the morning. He seemed to have got over his sulks; maybe it was the prospect of leaving for the beach tomorrow.

'I'm feeling much better, babe,' he said. 'Come over here, and I'll give you what you wanted earlier >'

I looked across at him with a desolate expression.

'I don't think I can, hon,' I said. 'I'm sorry but I'm a bit too saddle sore myself after today's ride. You'll have to wait until tomorrow.'

Golden Boy
by Landon Dixon

'This is Evan, father,' Patricia announced. 'The boy, er, young man I was telling you about.'

Clyde Spencer grunted, gripped the extended hand of the small, slender, blond-haired teenager. 'So you're the young man who's gotten my daughter's head all turned around.'

'Oh, Father!' Patricia scolded, her face flushing.

'Pleased to meet you, sir,' Evan responded warmly, clasping Clyde's big, blocky hand in both of his slim, brown hands, shaking. 'Patricia's told me a lot about you.' He grinned, his tanned, delicately-featured face beaming.

Clyde stared into Evan's bright blue eyes, his own face warming slightly at the other man's touch. He jerked his hand free, set the stern scowl more firmly on his blunt face. 'Patricia needs to get her business degree, not fool around with all this useless ... "art stuff".'

'Mother!' Patricia wailed.

'Let's all sit down at the table, shall we?' Isabel Spencer intervened. 'We're having roast beef for dinner, Evan.'

'Nothing formal,' Clyde added sourly, eyeing Evan's tight white T-shirt and faded blue jeans with disapproval.

'Sounds great!' the teenager enthused, squeezing Patricia's arm, eyes twinkling at Clyde.

'I just want to create art – beautiful things, is all, Mr Spencer,' Evan went on over dinner, as Clyde grilled him on his ambitions, or lack thereof, and his involvement with

Patricia.

'How about creating wealth, something to live on? Doing something productive with your life?' Clyde said, chewing sombrely on a piece of beef. Only in his mid-forties, the still stolidly handsome man looked older, his heavy features, the world-weariness reflected in his brown eyes, the grey strands streaking his otherwise brown hair, adding to that impression. Along with his staid, no-nonsense attitude.

'What's money, when there's no beauty? Money can't buy happiness, sir, or love.'

Patricia's violet eyes glowed at the young man. She had her mother's dark good looks, thick black hair combed straight back from her pale, oval face, her slender body sheathed in a thin, blue summer dress her mother had made for her. 'Evan's an artist,' she gushed. 'He wants to paint my picture – don't you, Evan?'

He looked at her and nodded.

'Nude, no doubt?' Clyde grumbled.

'Father!' both daughter and mother gasped.

'Not necessarily,' Evan said. 'Beauty isn't just skin-deep, after all.'

'And college isn't cheap. Tuition is an investment in future earnings, not a cover charge for good times.'

Evan laughed, softly, tilting his blond head back on his slim, bronze neck.

He went on eagerly chatting with Patricia and Isabel, about how he wanted to help people, bring more love and hope and beauty into the world. As Clyde devoured large quantities of roast beef and mashed potatoes and gravy, half-listening with a cynical smile on his thick lips.

'Kid should be called Pollyevan,' he remarked to his wife after dinner, as the pair sat in the living room reading the newspaper.

'I think he's sweet,' Isabel chided.

'You women! When –'

Clyde was interrupted by Evan and Patricia galloping

120

down the stairs from the second floor of the house.

'Evan's leaving!' Patricia sang out.

Clyde heaved himself to his feet, watching as Evan warmly hugged his wife. He extended his hand to the young man. Evan brushed by it, threw his arms around Clyde and hugged the older man just as warmly.

Clyde's face and eyes registered astonishment. Then something else, as he felt the pulsing heat of the 18-year-old's golden body. His hands hovered in mid-air, then dropped down on Evan's curved back, lower, sliding over and onto the young man's taut, rounded buttocks. His hands seemingly acting with a mind of their own.

And besides the beating excitement of Evan's hot body against his own, Clyde also felt the throb of the teenager's semi-erect cock against his own. The boy's eagerness and enthusiasm and warmth seemed to pour out of him into Clyde. The older man unconsciously clenched Evan's tight, mounded butt cheeks, a wonderful, tingling sensation flooding his own body and loins.

Evan pulled back, away, grinning. 'It was great meeting you, Mr Spencer. Hope to see you again.'

'Me ... too,' Clyde mouthed, as his daughter frowned at him, led her young friend outside.

Evan stayed over at the house two weekends later. His own parents were out of town at a wedding, and Patricia thought it would be a grand idea to invite him over. Clyde objected at first, but was quickly overruled by his wife and daughter.

Evan and Patricia spent most of the weekend working on a class project. While Clyde tried to get some of his own work done, client files he'd brought home from the office. It wasn't easy, with the constant stream of chatter and laughter coming from upstairs.

'This better not become permanent,' Clyde groused to his wife.

Isabel smiled, patiently sewing. 'I don't think you have to

worry about that, dear.'

But Clyde did worry, all that Saturday night and Sunday morning, tossing and turning in bed next to Isabel, thinking about young Evan asleep in the guestroom next door, reliving that rather intimate hug they'd shared. By six in the morning, he couldn't take any more, and rolled out of bed, dazed and angry.

He trundled down the hall to the bathroom, groaned when he heard water running in the shower. He stuck his head inside the cracked-open door and growled, 'Patricia, how long are you –'

But it wasn't his daughter monopolising the bathroom, as usual. It was Evan in the shower, the teenager's blond head and bronze shoulders sticking up above the glass door, the rest of his naked body outlined against the fogged glass. He was happily taking the jet of hot water full on his chest, his head tilted back, face and shoulders shining with moisture.

Clyde licked his lips, swallowed, watching Evan bathe. Everything the young man did seemed to be warm and sparkling and spirited. He rubbed his hands all over his chest, lower. Clyde coughed, and Evan turned his head.

'Oh sorry!' he called out over the steamy hiss of the water. 'I thought I'd grab a quick shower before everyone else wanted into the bathroom.'

He smiled brightly at Clyde, then turned off the taps, opened the shower door and stepped onto the bathmat – brilliantly, blazingly naked, seemingly unselfconscious of his gleaming golden body.

Clyde stared at the smooth, narrow chest, the puffy tan nipples, the taut stomach, the boyish hips. He just couldn't help himself – his gaze drifted lower, down Evan's flat lower stomach and into the matted blond fuzz of his groin, along the smooth, cut length of the young man's cock, down the slender, shapely legs to the dainty pair of feet.

Clyde's eyes lifted back up, to Evan's cock. He was surprised – and pleased – to see that it had engorged ever so slightly. Like his own cock in his thin, green pyjama bottoms.

'Can you hand me a towel, Clyde?'

The boy's voice was soft, thick like the air. Clyde picked a bath towel off the rack and walked right inside the bathroom, up to Evan, tingling with strange, heady emotion.

Evan turned around, said over his shoulder, 'Got my back?'

Clyde gazed down the boy's femininely curved back, stared at the lush pair of buttocks swelling up from his bottom. He draped the towel over Evan's shoulders, hardly breathing, and rubbed. Rubbed lower, and lower.

'That feels good,' Evan murmured, wiggling his bum slightly as Clyde engulfed it with the towel.

He rubbed the golden swells of the boy's buttocks, the towel draping still lower, revealing more and more cheek. Until it dropped right out of Clyde's trembling hands, and he filled those perspiring hands with Evan's bare, brown cheeks, grasping, squeezing, plying the burnished flesh.

Evan looked back at the man, his blue eyes shining and body arching, bum thrusting out further into Clyde's gripping and groping hands.

Clyde just couldn't help himself. The boy's buttocks felt just as exquisite as they looked, plushly cuppable things to be captured and caressed. He gazed down at them, transfixed, hands kneading and kneading, body burning.

The steamy spell was only broken when Evan suddenly turned around and kissed the older man softly on the lips. 'Thanks,' he breathed into Clyde's startled face.

Clyde saw the boy's cock, jutting out now directly at him, tanned and smooth as the rest of the teenager, but no mistaking the masculinity. He stumbled backwards, staggered out of the bathroom and down the hall to his bedroom.

'Oh, Clyde!' Isabel murmured into her pillow, as she felt her husband's hard, yearning cock press in between her

123

buttocks.

Clyde fucked his wife with an awesome ferocity.

A week later, Patricia invited Evan out to the family cottage.

'That boy's got an artist's technique for mooching, all right,' Clyde groused, watching Evan and his daughter splash around in the sun-dappled lake from the comfort of his deck.

'They have a lot in common,' Isabel said, leafing through a magazine.

'Humph,' Clyde grunted. 'I assume they're sharing all they have too, are they?'

Isabel looked up. 'Well ... I'm not sure. I've never actually caught them ... you know.'

The expression on Clyde's face brightened slightly under the warm summer sun.

Mother and daughter went to a movie in town that night, leaving "the boys" all by themselves. Evan sketched in the guest bedroom while Clyde barricaded himself behind a newspaper in the main room of the cottage, then fell asleep from exhaustion. It had been a difficult week for the man, dealing with his strange new feelings.

He was awakened by the light touch of fingers on his shoulders, gently massaging his muscles. 'Huh? What? You back from the movies already, honey?'

He glanced blearily at his watch, then at the hands on his broad shoulders. They were slender, elegant hands, with slim, sensitive fingers. But they weren't his wife's, they were Evan's.

'Just thought I'd return the rubdown, Clyde,' the young man breathed from behind Clyde's chair, fingers probing, kneading.

Clyde was suffused in shimmering warmth, the boy's touch feeling so good. The newspaper slipped out of his trembling hands as Evan slipped into his lap.

The beautiful teenager was as completely nude as he'd

been that morning in the bathroom, his bronze body glowing in the light from the tableside lamp, smelling as fresh and clean as the surrounding forest outside, hot with the heat of the night, and the depth of his passion. He slid an arm around Clyde's thick neck, draped his lithe legs over the chair, his bum pressing down into Clyde's groin, cock jutting out and up.

'Comfortable?' Evan asked, looking into the older man's dazzled eyes.

Clyde opened his mouth to say something, to put a stop to the foolishness, but no words came. His right arm coiled around Evan's waist, his left hand sliding up the boy's legs, fingers closing around the shaft of Evan's cock.

They both gasped, burning, buzzing, the pounding of their hearts obliterated by the beating of Evan's cock in Clyde's hand. They kissed, softly, warmly, wetly. Their tongues touched, swirled together.

Clyde couldn't think straight, didn't want to think. Evan was light in his arms, in his lap, on top of the throbbing erection that had swelled up between Clyde's legs. The boy's tongue was moist and pink and delightful, dancing against Clyde's tongue. The young man's hard cock thundered in Clyde's big, pumping hand.

Evan slipped one of his hands inside the open neck of Clyde's shirt and onto the man's broad, heaving chest. Clyde jerked when stroking fingers strummed his hardened pink nipples, groaned when Evan captured his outstretched tongue between plush lips and sucked on it.

Then the boy was up in Clyde's arms, the older man cradling him, carrying him off to the bedroom he and his wife shared. He set Evan gently down on the bed, then stood there looking down at the laid-out young man, as he stripped off his own clothes. The blond smiled warmly, his eyes hooded, naked caramel body stretched out, an erotic work of art.

Evan welcomed Clyde into his arms. The two men

clasped one another, their bare bodies melding together, Clyde's turgid pink erection pressing against Evan's tanned hard-on, making them one. They French-kissed, their cocks sliding together.

Clyde's head spun, his body ablaze. He urgently tasted the young man, squeezing him tight, fucking his cock against Evan's. It seemed only natural when Evan rolled him over, then squirmed around and straddled Clyde's head, cock dangling down to the older man's open mouth.

Clyde hesitated on the threshold, dazed, until he felt Evan grasp and lift his cock and subsume his hood and shaft in wet, warm pleasure, suck on it. Then Clyde hungrily sucked up Evan's mushroomed hood, half the pulsating shaft, digging his fingers into the boy's lush butt cheeks and bobbing his head up and down, eagerly blowing Evan like Evan was blowing him.

Clyde's throat loosened up like the rest of him, and he took Evan's cock deeper and deeper inside, revelling in the feel of the engorged appendage sliding back and forth between his lips, along his tongue, getting his mouth and throat filled. As Evan sucked equally deep, equally passionately on Clyde's cock.

Time had no meaning, the outside world obliterated. Just a beautiful boy and his cock, in Clyde's arms and mouth.

He wasn't the least bit surprised at his joy, when Evan rolled on his back on the bed and whispered, 'Fuck me, Clyde.'

There was lube tucked away in a cupboard in the headboard. Clyde scrambled up on his knees, at Evan's bum. The young man raised his legs, pressed his thighs into Clyde's chest. Evan slickened Clyde's raging dong with a few strokes of his hand, then his own smooth crack, his pretty pink pucker. He raised his butt up off the bed, presenting Clyde with his starfish, the stunning sight of his tightened balls and stretching cock.

Clyde swallowed, looking at the boy's ass and cock, into

Evan's shining eyes and face. Then he gripped his glistening dick and pushed the bloated tip against Evan's pucker.

They both jumped. Clyde bit his lip, pushed harder. He watched in dizzy amazement, as his meaty hood popped through Evan's pink rim, was swallowed up in the young man's anus.

Clyde groaned, and thrust. His vein-knotted shaft sunk into Evan's chute, the hole he filled for the very first time tighter and hotter than any woman's pussy. His hairy balls kissed up against Evan's smooth cheeks, the men joined.

Evan pulled one of Clyde's gripping hands off his thigh and placed it on his cock. Clyde pumped his hips, fucking the boy, pulling on the boy's cock. Evan whimpered and plucked at his nipples, staring up at the man earnestly churning his chute.

Clyde was on fire. He'd never felt such searing pleasure. He looked down at his cock pistoning another man's ass, at the other man's erection he was wildly tugging on in rhythm to his pumping cock. He fucked faster, harder, driving the both of them past the limit, unconscious with the wicked, white-hot sensations.

Evan cried out, his cock jumping in Clyde's hand. Semen spurted out the tip, striping the boy's face and chest, powerful blasts of ecstasy the direct results of Clyde's pumping hand and cock.

Clyde ploughed full length back and forth in Evan's spasming anus. Then erupted himself, shocked by equally powerful jolts of utter bliss, spouting semen deep into his Evan's ass.

They came together, over and over and over, all-out orgasm consuming the lovers.

Evan moved away to the coast with his parents later that summer.

'Do you still keep in contact with the boy?' Isabel asked her daughter over dinner one night, deep into the fall session of school.

Patricia looked up and shrugged. 'Evan? Not so much. Father was right, he simply wasn't practical – painting and drawing all the time.' She sniffed. 'Did I mention I got a 90 on my marketing mid-term?'

Clyde smiled absently at his daughter, chewing on a hunk of roast beef. He was thinking of his next "business" trip to the coast. Evan wanted to paint him – nude, of course.

Room 22
by Vick Guthrie

Another day. Another complaint. Joy. Today, number 20 complained about number 22, next door. Apparently they kept hearing noises, bangs late at night and lots of "moaning".

Brilliant. Another pervy customer to deal with. As the assistant manager of the hotel, it's always my responsibility to go and sort these things out. Shouldn't I be able to hire or even order someone to do it for me in my semi-managerial capacity?

I knocked once but there was no answer.

I knocked again, to double check, and there was still no response, so I got my keys out to go and investigate. 'Sorry, mister, if you make lots of noise, then you're going to have to deal with the consequences,' I grumbled under my breath.

Oh holy cow. The guy staying in 22 must have been having all-night orgies from the amount of stockings, tights and lacy underwear strewn about the room. 'More than one person staying in the room? That's certainly not allowed. I'll have to tell Marv.'

I really do feel sorry for our cleaners, having to touch such manky sheets, but I'm sure as hell not going to do it! Maybe I should really think about giving them gloves to wear. I supposed at least it didn't smell like a sweaty orgy had taken place. Not that I know what that would smell like anyway ...

I took in the state of the room. It looked dim and grotty in the dark. The curtains were shut and the dark red carpet was stained with patches of something sticky. A suitcase was in front of the open bathroom door, and as I stepped over to have a quick nose around, my heel caught the top of the case and the lid flew back against the floor.

Piled high in the case were stockings. Lots of them. A few stocking-themed pornos were lying alongside a single white pinstripe shirt and a bottle of deodorant. This guy was obviously seriously into his fetish. Not that I can judge. I'll take any chance to dress up in pretty undies and some suspenders.

I'd been in here way too long. The last thing I wanted was for some guy to walk in here and see me looking in his stuff.

After returning the case to its previous position, I returned to the reception desk, to ask Charlie to keep an eye out for "number 22" and to inform him that the assistant manager needed to speak to him.

Out of nowhere, a hottie waiting at the desk caught my eye. I turned and greeted him with my best smile.

'Hello, sir, welcome to Marvin's Hotel. How may I help?' I think I may have batted my eyelashes just a little too much.

Nevertheless, he smiled – with perfect white teeth, may I add – and I wanted to melt into a puddle right on the spot. Let's forget about the wetness that suddenly flooded my knickers.

'Hi, I was just wondering if I could have a few more towels in the morning, I seem to have run out.' His voice was like a purr. It rumbled gently, deep inside that gorgeous stubbly neck of his.

I actually had to tell myself to stay calm, collected, and act cool. 'Yes of course, Mr ...'

'Booth.'

'Mr Booth.' The name just rolled off my tongue, 'Which

room are you in?'

'Twenty-two.'

My breath caught and my eyes widened.

'Are you okay, Miss?' he asked, obviously wondering why I had gone silent.

'I ... Yes, thank you, Mr Booth. I was just trying to remember where that was.'

'An assistant manager who doesn't know her own hotel?' He smirked.

'How do you know I'm assistant manager?' I asked, eyebrow raised, curious about this handsome man who had an apparent stocking fetish and a bit of an attitude problem.

'It says so on your name tag, Miss Williams.' Mr Booth walked off and up the stairs to his room, leaving me irritated, but deliciously horny after our little encounter. Great arse, though. I definitely wanted me some of that.

So anyway, you won't *believe* what I did this morning. Even I'm not sure if I do!

Before the usual cleaner arrived, I sneaked into the cleaning cupboard, and donned the short, white dress that Jane usually wears. I pulled my favourite stockings from my bag and put them on, along with suspenders, leaving my discarded clothes on top of the mop bucket for later. Then I awkwardly wheeled the big cleaning trolley out of the cupboard and along the hall.

I knocked at number 22 but again, there was no answer. I sneaked in with my cleaning trolley. The longer I was in the room, the longer thoughts of what he must have been doing on his bed raced through my head. Orgies with six or seven women, tying them up, fucking them up the arse while bent over the end of the bed ... It was too much. I sat on the edge of the bed, spread my legs and circled my clit through the material of my knickers. My juicy pussy soaked my knickers and I was tempted to leave them on his floor to add to his collection. I did wonder if he'd even notice. I had a wank on his bed, knowing he could turn up at any second. I stuffed three fingers into my hole, and brought myself off to a hugely satisfying orgasm.

Suddenly, I heard the sound of the door opening and I shot to my feet, smoothing down my uniform, extremely conscious of the fact my fingers were wet and sticky from having been shoved up my cunt not ten seconds previously. Taking a few deep breaths, I turned and there stood Mr Booth, in dark blue trousers and the white pinstripe shirt, in his doorway.

'Can I help you?' He looked bemused.

'I'm here to clean and give you some more towels,' I said, looking flushed.

Mr Booth raised an eyebrow, his eyes immediately drawn to my legs. My stockings.

I wondered if he knew at that moment they were stockings. I wondered if he could see the lacy tops.

'Assistant manager who cleans her own hotel? What happened to the ginger lady who came around yesterday morning?'

'She called in sick,' I lied.

I fiddled with the bottles on the trolley for a moment, trying to find a duster and some polish. I took my time wiping the window ledge, the wardrobe, and the mirror. I wondered if he knew I was fibbing. I wondered if he knew I was there because I wanted to be fucked like the dirty little whore I am.

He sat down and stretched out across the bed on his front, typing away at his laptop, paying me no mind. He looked like a proper businessman. My brilliant "seduce the customer with my stockings" plan hadn't got off to a great start.

I stood at the corner of the bed nearest to his face and bent over, pretending to pick something off the floor. My bare pussy was exposed right in front of him but I had no idea if he noticed. I felt slightly disappointed as I stood back up that he didn't react.

But suddenly, a gentle finger brushed against my hairless lips and immediately slipped right up into my tight, hot wet pussy. I gasped in surprise ... Is it really surprise when I was practically begging it to happen, anyway?

I stood up and he pushed me face first against the wall, spreading my legs wide open and shoving his fingers deep inside me, his warm body pressed tightly against mine. His free hand reached around, grabbed at my white uniform, and the buttons flew off all over the room as he ripped it open. I spun around and my brain went into meltdown. His lips caressed my neck, biting teasingly before pressing forcefully against my mouth, kissing me deeply.

Before I knew it, I was on my dirty knees on the rough carpet, this stranger's cock begging entrance to my mouth. His skin smelt delicious. Musky, manly, with a hint of lime shower gel. His cock was perfect. That's not something you'll hear me say much – it was perfectly straight, just fat enough for the tips of my fingers to touch. I licked the dribble of salty precome from his leaky tip, but he couldn't wait for my teasing and pushed his prick inside my mouth. I took it all the way in and let him thrust into my mouth until my jaw started to ache.

My fingers found their way to his shaft, and I transferred my mouth to his clean-shaven balls. I took one at a time and rolled them gently in my mouth before sucking, and he gasped at me to stop – he wanted to fuck me before coming. My skin tingled with excitement, my pussy dripping wet in anticipation of feeling his cock inside me. He stood back from me for a moment, gazing down lustfully at my black, lacy stockings.

Not a single word was exchanged between us as he opened his trousers and we fucked against the wall. His thumb constantly rubbed at my swollen clit and within moments I was considering begging him to just let me come. I swear I'd never been so turned on before. I'd never been so wet or so ready to come within moments of touching.

He put his arms around me and picked me up, lying me down on the bed. I wanted to giggle as his hands fondled their way up my ticklish legs, his tongue making a long, wet trail up the inside of my stockinged legs. He rubbed his face against them, stopping when he reached my waiting pussy. It was begging to be touched. Begging to be licked and sucked and nibbled. I cried out loud as his tongue flicked over my clit and, almost instantly, I was coming.

He flipped me over on the bed, and rubbed his cock up and down my pussy. His hands gripped at my hips, pushing them down into the bed, and my heart skipped a beat as he slid his cock home. He wriggled his thumb into my virgin arsehole and I squealed in surprise – and pleasure. He thrust really hard and fast until we were both gasping, about to come, then pulled out.

My body was shaking with passion as he stroked my legs. Stroked my stockings. He ripped a hole in the inside of one and slid his cock into the hole, against my leg.

I squeezed my thighs together tightly and his eyes rolled back in his head.

He then rolled me back over on my back and straddled me, moving up my body to my chest, where he teased my nipples with the wet tip of his cock.

Grinning cheekily, I squeezed my boobs together for him. He smiled that sexy, cocky smile, and spat on his hand, using it to lube up his cock before sliding it between my boobs. I was desperate to lick the bulging head of his cock, but couldn't reach.

His breathing began to get heavy and I knew he was close as he reached for a stocking he had hidden under a pillow. I'm not sure if I want to know where it came from.

Wrapping it around his cock, I stroked him faster, moving the fabric over his skin, and he suddenly thrust uncontrollably into my hand, coming on the stocking, and over my breasts. As he regained his senses, he lay down next to me, his head in the crook of my neck, and rubbed his spunk into my chest, drawing patterns and swirls.

My watch alarm beeped insistently at me, spoiling the moment, and reminding me that Jane would be turning up for work soon.

I sat up, and scraped around on the floor for the ripped uniform. 'I have to go,' I mumbled, never very good with awkward moments like this.

'Miss Williams ...?'

I looked up, about to open the door.

'Can I have those extra towels, please?'

At first, I huffed in anger. The cheek of him. But after a few seconds, a laugh escaped my lips and I threw him some towels from the trolley. He smiled and winked at me before I left, holding my uniform together with one hand, and pushing the cleaning trolley with the other.

When I arrived back down at the main desk looking slightly more presentable, Charlie was waiting for me.

'Miss Williams,' he started, 'we've had another complaint this morning about the noise in number 22.'

Star-fucker
by Jade Taylor

I never was a star-fucker.

There was too many about in this business, too many bothered about their hair and their clothes, who they were photographing and whether they could fuck them, rather than the composition, the *art*.

But that was never me. You started thinking like that and your work suffered; you weren't considered a professional any more once you stopped being the one taking the photos and became the one in the photos, dressed in revealing outfits in the Sunday tabloids with Max Clifford on speed dial.

But kissing and telling had never been my thing.

Not that I ever had anybody famous to kiss and tell about; that just wasn't me.

That's partly why I got the job: discretion. I wouldn't sell out whomever I was photographing so that the paparazzi could gather outside like vultures looking for the dead. Whomever I photographed was between them, the camera and me.

Another was that I was getting good. Still young enough that I was finding my style, still brave enough to experiment, my commissions regularly coming from the edgier magazines.

And last, but not least, I seemed plain. I never saw the sense in dressing up for work, no make-up and flat shoes seeming much more practical, and nice clothes only getting ruined by the chemicals I use. Dressing up and fucking was for the weekend, and God knows I could find enough boys to play with *without* compromising my reputation.

So it was me, the anti-star-fucker, who the editor called.

But for every rule there's an exception, and he was mine.

I couldn't tell her that it was different this time; that there was one star I'd love to fuck.

Sure, we all knew his reputation, the bragging about how much he could drink and the women he'd bedded – no doubt she thought I was level-headed enough to take it all in my stride, brush him off like other women seemed unable to. Or maybe she thought he wouldn't want me in my flat shoes and thick-rimmed glasses, appearance screaming not to touch.

But she'd never seen me glammed up.

She didn't know that when I wasn't in my dark-room I was at the gym, that while baggy T-shirts and many-pocketed combats were ideal work-wear, I preferred a sexy dress and high heels away from my job.

She didn't know that I was mad about him, that I'd been fantasising about him for as long as I could remember.

You could keep all the other mega-stars; the vain actors more bothered about being photographed from the "right" side than the person behind the camera, the action heroes who wore more make-up than I did, the sexy singers so full of angst they had no room for anything else; they did nothing for me.

But he was different.

I'd first seen him in some crappy daytime soap, his acting appalling but with looks you couldn't ignore; tall and dark-haired with those puppy dog eyes making you unsure whether you wanted to mother him or fuck him first. The broad shoulders, the narrow waist, that tight, tight bottom.

It didn't hurt that the soap required scenes of him stripping almost daily.

Back then it was a teenage crush, adolescent hormones looking for the likeliest target, our worlds never likely to meet. I was the girl in braces who found it easier to hide in a darkroom than talk to boys, back then a hobby that meant bullying rather than encouragement.

His acting got better and he moved to prime-time TV – fewer scenes with unnecessary stripping and more magazine interviews with glossy photo spreads. Then he moved to Hollywood, somehow bypassing the "best friend who gets killed" roles and straight to the romantic lead, those smouldering eyes finally put to better use.

And now *I* was to take those photos that would promote his latest film.

I couldn't stop thinking about him.

Every night as I lay in my bed my hand went between my legs, and instead of planning what photos I would take, of how to make mine different from the rest, I plan what I want to do to him.

The photos of him these days arc all glossily seductive, him dressed in a smart suit, sexy but sophisticated, suave and handsome.

That's not what I want.

I want the raw sexiness that all his admirers know is there underneath the gloss, the cheekiness that's so appealing laid bare. I want it to be blatantly obvious in my photos.

I'm not sure if this is what my editor wants. The rack of beautifully cut suits she has sent over to my studio suggests not, but I know that she trusts my talent, that though I'm almost obsessed by the thought of having him, I'm not blinded by lust; that this will work.

I get a bed moved in to my studio, the difficulty of doing so more than outweighed by the thought of him in it. I make it up with crisp white sheets, knowing how good his olive skin will look against it. I lie in it touching myself, imagining him lying naked beside me, wishing my hands

139

were his.

He walks in with his entourage like he owns the place, not even deigning to introduce his people as they spread out around my work area, taking over like locusts, too busy fiddling with his phone to say a word to me.

'And these are?' I ask, gesturing around the room.

'Hair, make-up, publicist, assistant, stylist,' he says in an off-hand way, still doing something on his phone, as if everyone should expect to walk around with such people, and he's so blasé that however attractive he may be, I'm already furious with him.

'Aren't you big enough to do this on your own?' I ask, stepping closer to get into his space, determined to get his attention. He might be used to women being in his personal space, but he's more used to them fawning over him, not getting ready to blow a fuse.

His eyes meet mine for the first time, and he smiles, that lazy million dollar smile that's made him famous throughout the world.

I don't smile back.

He holds it for a minute, waiting for me to cave, but I don't; he's fucking gorgeous but I'm fucking stubborn.

He steps back and stops smiling.

'Okay gang, the lady wants us to have a little privacy, so you all want to go find a coffee shop or something to entertain yourselves with?'

A small mousey man steps closer and starts to whisper in his ear, but he maintains eye contact with me and brushes away whatever the man is saying.

'No, I've been told she's the best so let's go with it.'

I don't know if he's being genuine or he hopes this blatant flattery will calm me down, but I don't care; I'm too focused on the job at hand to care.

'Your hair and make-up look fine to me, and I do my own styling,' I tell him dismissively, and his group file away as he starts to flick through the suits that have been sent over.

'So what did you have in mind?' he asks, holding up a light grey suit against his body. It would look stunning, he automatically knows what would suit him, but it's not what I had envisaged.

'I was thinking of something more ... dishevelled,' I tell him, taking the suit from him and putting it back on the rail. I lead him through to the back of my studio, to where the bed is.

'Why, Miss, I'm really not that kind of boy,' he jokes, and now I laugh too; he's finally put the phone away and it seems the bed has got his attention.

'That's not what I've heard.' I laugh. 'And I thought we could shoot something based on that reputation.'

For a moment he stops, obviously considering it, making me realise he's not as dumb as the media have made out. 'My people wouldn't like it,' he tells me, but that's not a no.

'And what about you?'

'Let's see how it goes.'

'OK. So how about barefoot and shirt unbuttoned for the first shot, lying on the bed like you've just got in from a long night out?' I ask, checking my cameras are set up properly as he slips off his shoes and socks and quickly poses on the bed.

He follows directions well, and I'm all professionalism behind the camera, judging the best way for him to move and altering the lights accordingly, trying to forget what I want to do next, ignore who exactly it is I have lying on a bed in front of me.

Ignore the heat pulsing between my legs.

It doesn't help that now he only has me to look at I can feel his eyes upon me. Today I'm not in a T-shirt and combats; instead, I've dressed for the occasion in a fitted white shirt and black pencil skirt, aiming for the sexy secretarial look.

The way I feel his eyes undressing me I can tell he appreciates the look.

Which is good, as next I ask him, 'Could you open your shirt?'

He raises an eyebrow, sexily maintaining eye contact as he slowly unbuttons his shirt.

I hide behind my camera. I'm wet already and want him so much, but I know I need to focus a little longer at least.

His chest is more toned than it seemed in his younger shots; he's more muscular, more manly, with a light covering of chest hair. Those younger shots seemed to make him out to be more boy-band material. Now he seems more masculine, less refined and more sexual.

I like it.

When he smiles I realise I'm blushing, my thoughts written across my face as easy to read as saying them aloud.

I turn away, pretending I'm adjusting something on my camera as I ask, 'How about losing the shirt and trousers?'

He pulls off his shirt completely, then starts to open his jeans before stopping and saying, 'I don't have underwear on.'

I want to laugh; neither do I today.

Instead I tell him, 'The sheet's there to protect your modesty.'

I keep my back turned until I hear the moving and rustling stop, and then I turn back, my heart in my mouth.

I don't know if my pulse is beating harder in my chest or between my legs.

He's naked, the duvet thrown casually across him, as if this were some lazy Sunday morning in bed, not a high-profile photo shoot.

He smiles at me, and I shoot off some pictures quickly, hiding behind my camera once more.

Then I don't want to hide any more.

'How do you feel about making this a little more risqué?'

'What did you have in mind?' he asks, sitting up slightly,

142

the sheet slipping down his toned abs, making my pulse quicken.

'Handcuffs,' I tell him, fetching them out of my bag of props. He looks hesitant. 'If you want to?'

'How can I resist an offer like that from such a sexy lady?' he laughs, but still looks apprehensive as I fasten his left wrist to the headboard. 'Do I need a safe word?'

'Do you think you need one?' I ask, leaning over him, my breasts barely inches from his face as I fasten his right wrist just as quickly.

'No,' he says, moving slightly to get closer.

I pause for a moment, letting him brush his lips against me, then move away, watching as he pulls lightly at his restraints.

'Anyone would think you're trying to take advantage of me,' he laughs.

'I'm just trying to photograph you in a different way,' I tell him, stepping back behind my camera and rattling off a few shots. 'If I were going to take advantage of you, then maybe I'd do something like this ...'

I walk back to the bed and, facing the foot of the bed, straddle him. I push the sheet down, and slowly lean forward and lick his hard cock. He sighs, and I know he can see straight up my skirt, that I'm naked beneath my skirt, must be able to see how wet I am for him.

I wriggle my hips, and my skirt is so tight that it quickly rides up, fully exposing my nakedness for him to see.

'If I wasn't tied up right now,' he starts, then says nothing as I move back and he uses his mouth on me.

He has a talented tongue, and as I lick at his slippery cock and then take it in my mouth it's hard to maintain a rhythm, hard to focus on what he likes as his tongue laps at my clit, driving me wild. It's hard to believe I have one of the most desirable men in the world handcuffed to my bed and licking at my cunt, even as the pressure builds, even as I suck at him harder and faster as my orgasm takes me over.

He groans as I stop sucking at him and climb off the bed.

'Hey, what about me?'

'What about you?' I say, pulling up the sheet to make him look decent once more as I pick up my camera.

He looks pissed off but also amused and confused, and overwhelmingly sexy. He looks horny and frustrated and full of sensuality.

The pictures are amazing.

I want to fuck him so badly. I know it's a bad idea, that the more I do the more chance there is I'm wrecking a career I love so much, but the fact that I shouldn't be doing this just makes it even more appealing.

'You want some too?' I ask, reaching in my bag now for a condom before I change my mind.

His eyes light up, and he looks so perfect I almost wish I hadn't put down the camera.

Almost.

I quickly put the condom on and climb on top of him. He slides inside me easily; I'm wet and slick and ready for him, and start moving immediately, my hips moving in the rhythm I need. He moans in enjoyment, his hands pulling against the cuffs and I know that if his hands were free right now he'd be grabbing me to move the way he wanted. But he can't; I'm in control now, and I like it.

I lean forward to kiss him, tasting myself on him, his tongue meeting mine for the first time, sending a charge of electricity through me. I grind against him, moving slowly and feeling him deep inside me, and though he moves his hips, tries to make me speed up, I take my time, rubbing my body against his, kissing him hard and sighing as I come hard once again.

This time when I move away from the bed he lets loose with a stream of expletives.

'Temper temper,' I laugh, picking up my camera once more, taking some photos I know I'd need to edit later, his cock still on display, but looking so hot and angry and aroused I don't want to stop right now.

'Please, I feel like I'm about to explode,' he moans.

'You're left-handed, yes?'

'Yes,' he replies, obviously confused.

I unlock the handcuff on his left wrist, then dance out of the way quickly before he can grab me.

'There we go then, if you're that desperate.'

He laughs. 'You're seriously unfair, I've made you come twice and you won't even make me come once?'

'Nope,' I tell him. 'But maybe I could give you some encouragement.'

His eyes widen as I slowly undo my shirt, showing off the black and red bra underneath, low cut so my breasts are almost spilling out.

His eyes widen, fixed on my breasts, his hand almost unconsciously going toward his dick.

I pull my skirt up again, showing him my wet cunt, showing him how turned on he makes me, then as I slowly start to tease myself, his hand finally grips his cock hard.

I watch him stroking his cock, hesitantly at first, then more rapidly, eyes going from my face, to my almost exposed breasts, to my fingers stroking my clit.

He watches me as I get closer once more, as I start sighing, my other hand going to my breasts, playing with my nipples through the flimsy material of my bra.

It's too much, and he cries out, jerking on the bed, his cock spurting thick come all over his toned abs. I come too, this last orgasm more intense than the others, leaving me trembling all over.

I throw him the handcuff key and quickly head to the back room, scared of what happens next.

When I return I'm in my combats and old T-shirt, and he is fully dressed. He laughs at my change of outfit.

'You think that would put me off?' he asks, moving closer to me, backing me up against the wall then pinning me against it to kiss me hard.

I melt beneath his touch, flooded with desire for him again, even though I've climaxed more times than I thought I could so quickly.

He moves away, leaving me clinging to the wall for support, my legs weak.

'I'd like to call you sometime.'

'I'm sure your people have my card.'

'That's not quite what I meant.'

'I don't date my subjects.'

'You just fuck them?'

I blush.

'Not usually.'

'I'll call you,' he says, kissing me again.

He does call me, but I find it easier to stick to my principles when I'm not seeing him face to face. We flirt, but we don't meet, and I try to forget about that mad night that should have never happened.

It makes it harder that the photos are so popular.

They're replicated everywhere, praised for bringing out his raw sensuality, for their sexiness, their *edge*.

The photos I don't publish could earn me a fortune, but they're for me, for my private collection.

Without them I could believe that night was pure fantasy.

With them I believe that the fantasy could happen again.

Working Late
by Heidi Champa

The office building was dark, just a few offices lit by the cleaning crews that came in at night. The hum of a vacuum cleaner in the distance was the only noise I could hear, other than the blood pounding in my ears. My body felt like it was vibrating, an electric current running in my veins instead of blood. The elevator opened, and I stepped into the light. The mirrored walls showed me my reflection, the dilated pupils and flushed face of someone who was about to be fucked. I pressed a hand to my neck, feeling the warmth coming off my skin. There was no turning back now. My elevator arrived on the proper floor, closing behind me with a slight creak. I strode down the hall to my husband's office; a route I had taken a million times before. But my husband wasn't there.

I pushed open the door, the office completely dark. I could make out the shadows of his furniture, the heavy lines of the desk and sofa that made up the floor plan. Just as I pressed the heavy wooden door closed, the banker's lamp on the desk sprang to life, scaring me. I was expecting him to be there, but the jolt of light still made jump. His voice was rough, the expression on his face obscured by darkness.

'You're late.'

I coughed, wondering if my voice would still work with my heart in my throat.

'I'm sorry. I didn't mean to keep you waiting.'

I moved toward him, only getting a few feet closer before he stopped me.

'Stay right there. I didn't tell you to move.'

Frozen, I felt every muscle tighten, trying to do as he asked. My purse was still in my hand, my fingers struggling to hold on to its weight. The seconds ticked by, my breathing ragged as I waited.

'Take off your coat and put your purse down.'

I was able to relax for a moment as I shrugged off my trench and laid it carefully over the arm of the couch. I set my purse on top of it, and turned my attention back to him. He started drumming his fingers on the large calendar that sat on the desk, the impatient rhythm causing a bead of sweat to trickle between my breasts. He leaned forward, his face finally visible to me. His eyes moved up and down my body, my trembling becoming uncontrollable. I kept my eyes glued to his face, but I took a small bit of pleasure at the smile that broke across his lips when he saw my fishnet-covered legs.

'Open up that blouse. Show me your tits.'

I had followed his instructions carefully, making sure every detail was just right. The blouse I was unbuttoning was one he had chosen for me, the silk caressing my skin, as he strictly forbid me to wear a bra. Dropping the fabric to the floor, the cool, processed air of the office blew across my nipples. They were already hard from anticipation, but now they were bordering on painful.

'Now the skirt.'

The black skirt he had bought me hugged my hips, the hemline just a little too short for my usual conservative tastes. But he wanted me to wear it, so I did. I had no choice. Underneath, my pussy was bare. In addition to being told not to wear panties, he had instructed me to get myself waxed. I was to be completely hair free, and my naked pussy lips were already slick and wet as I pushed the skirt to the floor and stepped out of it. All that remained were the thigh-high fishnet stockings and the stiletto heels he had sent me the week before. I stood before him, my hands at my sides, obediently.

'God, what a slut you are. Coming all the way across town with no panties on. I hope you kept your legs crossed in the cab.'

He stood up and walked toward me; each footfall slow and deliberate. My eyes followed him, but I remained still, knowing if I didn't, there would be trouble. He stood right in front of me, towering over me, even with the extra height my shoes provided. Resting a hand on my shoulder, I let out a deep breath. I had been waiting for him to touch me all week, ever since the new instructions had come. As his hand crept lower, I was desperate to arch my back, to move my aching nipple closer to his hand, but I didn't dare.

'You've followed my instructions well. Good girl. Do you think you deserve a reward?'

'Yes, sir.'

My voice was soft, demure. He required it, and I loved it. I dropped my eyes when I spoke, acknowledging his power over me. I knew he liked it, and I didn't want to disappoint him after he had paid me a lovely compliment. His thumb and finger touched my nipple, gently stroking at first, teasing a moan out of my lips. Then a sharp pinch shot pain and heat through my body, my pussy getting wetter as I rode the wave of agony mixed with a shot of ecstasy. I tried to stifle the whimper from leaving my lips, but I couldn't. Just when I thought I couldn't bear another moment of torture, he released me. But, I barely had time to catch my breath before my other nipple was suffering the same fate, this squeeze even harder than the first. My knees started to buckle, but I fought to stay as still as I could. Deciding I had suffered enough, he let go, the blood rushing back into my nipple. He dipped his head, sliding his hot tongue over my recently abused flesh, the pain subsiding as it was replaced by the sucking pull of his mouth. I arched up into him, letting my hands fall on his shoulders. As soon as I touched him, he pulled away, roughly grabbing my wrists.

'You just never learn, do you?'

'I'm sorry, sir. Please, I didn't mean to.'

'Too late.'

I knew better than to touch him without permission, but I did it anyway. As much as I wanted him to fuck me, sometimes I desired his punishment more. Dragging me over to my husband's neat and orderly desk, he pushed me forward on to it, pressing his hand into the back of my neck to make me stay still. He kicked my feet apart, spreading my legs wider. I struggled just a bit, because I couldn't help myself, but I gave up as soon as the first smack hit my ass. He spanked me four more times, a fast flurry of strikes that made me cry out into the dark. After he stopped, I was stilled and silent, the only sound in the room his heavy breathing.

'What am I going to do with you, Linda? This was supposed to be a nice night for us. I sent your husband out for a long dinner with clients, so we could be alone, and I buy you those beautiful clothes, and you still disobey the rules.'

'I'm so sorry, sir.'

He spanked me some more, the pain of each slap radiating all through my body. I could feel my wetness dripping down my thigh as I moved back into each hit, relishing the power in his fury. He stopped again, this time putting a hand on my hip, stopping me from rocking back on my tall heels.

'See, now why don't I believe you, Linda? You're always pushing me, just so I'll punish you.'

'I swear, sir. I didn't mean to upset you.'

'Oh, I'm not upset. Because you're going to make it up to me, right now.'

He pulled me back to standing, my wrists still in his hands. Breathing into my ear, his voice was barely above a whisper.

'If I let you go, are you going to be a good girl, or do I have to tie you up?'

'I'll be good, sir. I promise.'

Letting me go, he spun me quickly, pushing me down on to my knees in front of him. I stared up at him as he tore of his shirt, throwing his tie aside before he put a hand to his belt buckle.

'What are you waiting for, slut? Open up my pants and get my cock in your mouth.'

The words cut right through me, a fresh wash of heat overtaking my body. I tried to steady my hands as I fumbled with the leather belt, finally getting his suit pants open. I pulled his boxers down his muscled legs and his cock sprang free. Opening my mouth, I took the head inside, running my tongue across the flared tip. I took him in slowly, feeling every bump and ridge play over my tongue. He didn't seem to like my pace, and grabbed a handful of my hair and pulled me back.

'I said suck it. Quit playing around, Linda, or you'll be sorry. Now suck it.'

This was exactly what I was hoping he would do. Forced down on to his cock, I relaxed my throat and took him all inside, letting him control me, use me the way he liked. I left my hands at my sides, even though he hadn't asked me to, letting him fuck my face. Saliva started to dribble down my chin, the crude noises coming from my mouth turning me on. Tears pricked the corners of my eyes, the force of his thrusts testing my gag reflex. I heard him grunting above me, and I thought for a moment he might finally come in my mouth. But, soon enough, he left my mouth, moving quickly to shuck off his pants while I waited for his next instructions.

'Get up.'

He practically growled as I rose to my feet, carefully placing my stilettos on the carpet. I moved to lean over the desk once more, placing my hands on the calendar that covered my husband's work area. I looked down at his meticulous writing, each block printed so perfectly. But, he reached out and stopped me, turning me to face him.

'No, not like that, Linda. Lie back and put those feet in the air.'

I put my ass on the edge, letting myself fall back onto the perfectly appointed desk. I pictured my husband at the fancy dinner across town, his perfectly pressed tied tucked into his shirt, so as not to chance a stain. He was the type that would be more upset at the idea of me messing up his desk than me getting fucked on it. I felt the press of his cockhead on my slit, moving up and down my wet cunt, but not trying to enter me. My ankles were in his hands, my legs spread obscenely wide. I tried to get him inside me, but it didn't do anything but crinkle the paper underneath my ass.

'What's the matter, Linda? Am I not moving fast enough for you? If you want me to fuck that sweet, wet pussy, I'm going to need to hear you beg me nicely.'

Beg. There was something about the word beg that melted my insides and turned me right into the slut he wanted me to be.

'Please, sir. I need you so bad. Please, fuck me.'

'Come on, Linda. You can do better than that.'

I groaned and whimpered, my body desperate for him, my brain boiling with need. Again, I moved, hoping to urge him on, but again I was denied. He just laughed, enjoying my undoing far too much.

'Please, sir. I'll be a good girl, I promise. I'll do whatever you want. Just fuck me. Fuck me, please.'

I fully expected more waiting, more torturous minutes of unrequited need. But, instead, he was inside me, his cock finally buried to the hilt. My pussy clenched around him, as he pumped into me slowly, my body not wanting to let him go. I looked up at him, his face the picture of concentration, a bit of sweat forming on his forehead. Leaning forward, he pressed my legs higher and wider, so he could thrust into me deeper and harder. As he fucked me, things started to fall from the desk, the force shaking loose his nameplate and the stapler that had been sitting by my head.

'Play with your nipples, Linda. Pinch them nice and hard for me.'

I moved my hands to my chest, rubbing and teasing my nipples for a moment before applying the hard pressure I knew he wanted to see. He fucked me faster, his thumb moving over my clit, gently rubbing small circles over my tight bud.

'Harder, Linda. Pinch those nipples harder.'

I obeyed, just like I always did, hurting myself because he wanted me to. I was rewarded with sweet strokes on my clit, his cock still moving in a steady, pounding pace. I wanted to come so bad, but it remained elusive. He knew what I needed to hear, but he wasn't going to give it to me yet. Again, I broke the rules, but I couldn't help myself. I just hoped he would take pity on me.

'Please, sir. I need to come.'

Instead of chiding me for not being patient, or worse, I was surprised when I heard his voice crack as he replied.

'Come for me, my little slut. I want you to come now.'

As soon as his permission was out of his mouth, my body responded. The orgasm that had been just out of reach was let free and I screamed out in my husband's office, coming around another man's cock, being fucked senseless right there on his desk. He didn't let up, fucking me hard as I let swell after swell of joy wash over me. When he finally came, he collapsed on top of me, letting out a possessive roar as he finished.

We were both sweaty and spent, neither of us keen to move. But finally, he rose, moving quickly, his lost composure back in an instant. We dressed in silence and after I closed the last button on my blouse, I set about the task of putting my husband's desk back in order. Once everything was in its place, he turned me around and kissed me hard, his fingers digging ever so slightly into my shoulders.

'So, until next time, Linda?'

'When will I see you again?'

He looked at my husband's calendar, then back at me.

'It seems he has a late meeting next week. How about then?'

'Don't you have to go too?'

'Nope.'

'Lucky you.'

'Hey, sometimes it's good to be the boss.'

Rule Breakers
by Rachel Kramer Bussel

In theory, what we are doing right now, at 2:34 in on a Tuesday afternoon, is supposed to be OK. There are rules, and technically we are abiding by them – or we would be, if we'd let Serena in on our little secret. But Rob, Serena's husband of five years, and I haven't let her in on anything, so instead, we are sprawled out on their marital bed while she is at work, and we are very much not working, unless you count his tongue buried in my pussy and my lips bobbing up and down on his cock "work". I don't; I consider this pure pleasure, the kind of bliss that makes pesky everyday things like rules melt away.

'Just forget about her for right now,' he'd said the first time it happened, when I'd stopped by to drop off some brownies I'd baked for my curvy girlfriend – her favourite kind, dusted with cayenne, giving them a hint of spice – and wound up kissing him. With her fire-engine red hair (though sometimes it's a shocking blue or purple, just to mix things up), Serena is the type of woman who likes spice, which is why she's always insisted on having an open relationship with Rob, even though I'm pretty sure he'd be just as happy to have her all to himself. He's more of the quiet, intellectual type, his bookshelves filled with Dickens, or maybe a political treatise he'd read about in the *New York Times Book Review*. He's the type who you can never guess what they're thinking until they speak, whereas Serena is the very opposite; she has no poker face whatsoever. She was the one with the ravenous appetite – for food, for sex, for life – the one who could never resist a locked door or "do not enter" sign, who was always restless unless she was shaking up the status quo. Sometime I was surprised she'd ever gotten married at all, but she'd told me over and over how Rob had seduced her in every way, how he was game for anything, how he had the biggest cock she'd ever seen – or tasted.

The thing is, when she started dropping hints about him, I became curious, and then more than curious. How could I not when she talked about him in such rapturous tones? Her giddiness was replaced with something else, an almost wistful tone, her cheeks pink with her own ardour. She wasn't shy about bragging about Rob, and didn't mind my increasingly probing questions, not even when we were in bed.

'Oh, he likes it when I use these clamps on his nipples,' she said once, laughing as she dangled them in the air, then attached them to my nubs. The more of these little morsels she shared, when we were out at the movies, where her fingers inevitably wound their way up my skirt and into my panties, or at a restaurant, where she'd tell me his favourite drink, the more I wanted to get to know this quiet man who'd shacked up with, married, partnered with such a glam, gorgeous woman. Did he revel in her outrageous flirting the way I did, or was he ever jealous? Did he like being the calm to her storm? I love Serena, in my own way; how could I not? She is the essence of a party girl, and she is always looking for, and finding, a good time.

But there is only so much of that wildness I could take before I wanted to know the man who was the yin to her yang, and that day, something about how he looked in his rumpled shirt – he's a writer who works from home, and he'd been taking a nap – made me want to ravish him, to taste him, to see which one of them I most resembled. Was I the quiet one waiting patiently for Serena to come home, or would I, with him, take on her role and overtake him? I was on my lunch hour, so I didn't have long, but I felt maybe a little of what she feels when she looks at him, this need to shake him up, to run my fingers through his messy hair, to rip the buttons off his shirt, to find out what lies beneath the surface.

'Oh – hi,' he said, startled even though I'd had to give my name at the door, then rise up thirty floors in the elevator of their high-rise building. I was bundled up for winter, my cheeks flushed by the cold, grateful for the added colour on my skin.

'I brought brownies,' I said, laughing, wondering if he noticed the tension in the room between us, a tension I'd never noticed before when the three of us had dinner or hung out and watched movies on their big-screen TV. 'You should try one,' I said, forcing a maturity, a command to my voice, that I wasn't really feeling.

'Sure,' he said, easy, casual, and moved toward the tin.

'No, let me,' I said, taking off my hat, scarf and coat and suddenly feeling overdressed in my navy pencil skirt and ivory silk blouse. I used the edge of one of my long nails to ease off the top of the tin, the smell of chocolate and spice wafting through the living room. I needed to do this my way, and my way, apparently, involved grabbing Rob and slamming him up against the front door. 'Close your eyes,' I said. 'They'll taste better that way.' I'd never touched the man before, had only fleetingly thought about his body when Serena had imparted something about the way he kissed or fucked or came; in those seconds, I'd get flashes of him naked, of his body spasming, his glasses off, his limbs quivering. I knew what Serena looked like in the throes of orgasm, but this, it was rapidly becoming clear, wasn't about Serena at all. Their home, zapped of her all-consuming energy, suddenly took on a life of its own.

His eyes were closed, and I broke off a corner of a

brownie, then brought it toward his lips. They were soft, thin and gentle, smooth as my fingers brushed against them and inserted the piece directly against his tongue. I reluctantly eased my fingers out and watched him, his eyes closed, his mouth processing the spice and the sweet. I couldn't recall what kind of eater he was, if his palate was mild, like his personality, or whether lurking inside was the kind of fiery tongue possessed by his wife. I kept my face close to his, letting him feel my breath against his lips, waiting until he was done. I didn't ask – not about what he thought about the brownie, or if he wanted me to press my lips against his; I just did it. You can tell if someone wants a kiss or not, if their lips yield to yours or not, if they sink into your passion or shrink away from it. Maybe our lips best express their intentions in their actions, rather than their words. A kiss can't lie, and this one certainly told the truth: Rob wanted me.

As my tongue traced his, catching hints of brownie, then going further, claiming Serena's husband's tongue as mine for this stolen moment, he answered me back. His tongue said, 'Yes, please, take me.' So I did; I shoved my tongue deep into his mouth, not thinking about Serena, but just feeling his body flush against mine. And that was how it started. That afternoon it was just a kiss; I had to leave, and I wanted to think about whether I was ready for this before jumping in fully.

He took care of the rest. By the time I got back to my office, there was an email from Rob ... with a photo of his hard cock. Then another a few minutes later showing me his come. I hadn't been with a guy since my last boyfriend; I'd met Serena and she'd been more than enough for me. Maybe he wasn't so mild, after all. I didn't miss cock per se, but I knew I couldn't say no to Rob; I suddenly missed him, needed him, and couldn't deny the way he made my whole body light up. Serena lit me up too, but if they didn't have to choose, why did I? Serena had a host of other lovers and, as far as I knew, Rob didn't.

I told him we'd wait a week, and if either of us changed our minds in the meantime, we wouldn't have to go through with it. 'Your wish is my command,' he wrote back. I found myself thinking about him all day, wondering about just how big his cock was, what kind of lover he was. I knew he was a sub to Serena, but was he always a sub, or would he be the type of guy to toss me on the bed, to bend me over and spank my ass until I screamed? I'm the type who gets so caught up in whoever I'm fucking at the moment that I forget about the parts of my sexuality that don't match up with them. Serena didn't like me to eat her pussy, so I didn't, but thinking about Rob, I realised my mouth was hungry, wet, eager to be filled. Sometimes she gave me her fingers to suck, or she had me open wide for one of her many dildos, but that wasn't the same. I get off on having my tongue on a lover's most intimate parts, on the slippery slide of a juicy pussy, of trying to capture all of it between my lips, or of the velvety hardness of a firm cock, straining for my tongue. I feel used in the best possible way when I am giving head, like I'm fulfilling my erotic destiny, and suddenly I couldn't wait to have Rob between my lips.

The day we are supposed to meet, I email him. 'I want your cock in my mouth, all of it.' I don't know for sure that I'll be able to take it all, but I don't care. I want it, want to prove to myself I can do it, I can take it. I saw Serena two nights ago and had to tell myself not to be disappointed when she pushed my head away from her pussy. She'd guided my fingers inside her, biting my lip as I slid four into her wetness, and she almost made me forget about her husband. Almost. But once she'd slipped out of my queen-sized bed, I lay there, a queen without any subjects.

Now I have one, or he has me; maybe we have each other. The day has gone by in a blur, and I like knowing Serena won't be home until much later; she's already

159

bragged to me about the threesome she's arranged with two hot studs. I am eager to get to my own hot stud, who is apparently craving the joy of going down as much as I am, so we have compromised and are in a sixty-nine position.

His cock is, indeed, enormous, but the way he is eating me, the noises he's making, the feel of his fingers digging into my hips and pulling me close, make my throat open so I can take him all the way down. We simply cannot get enough of each other, and though part of me wants to tell Rob all the things I've been thinking about him, all the ways I've been fantasising about him, all the dirtiest words I can think of, instead I wait, saying them silently in my head as I put all my energy into showing him with my mouth exactly how happy I am to be there.

'Wait,' he finally says, lifting me up, impressing me with his strength.

I laugh, tracing my tongue along his length. 'You don't like what I'm doing?'

'Oh, I like it plenty, so much that I'm worried I might come. Plus I want to see you,' he responds, turning me around so I'm on my back and pulling me close. I've been in their bed before, but this feels different, new, because it is. Maybe I should feel guilty, but though guilt tries to nip at the edges of my excitement, mostly I feel frisky, powerful, free as I shake my hair out around my shoulders, exulting in the sun shining through the window.

'You're beautiful,' he breathes reverently. I don't interrupt or argue that Serena is more beautiful, I just lean down and kiss him, aware of our limited time, both this afternoon and in general. Though I've never had one before, I know that affairs aren't for ever.

'No, you're beautiful.' I pull him up so I can stare at us in the mirror on the wall, then amend my statement. '*We're* beautiful.' And, in our way, we are. I'm so used to considering him next to her, to her omnipresence, that it's taken me a little while to think of him and me as an us, an entity, a pair who might be well-matched.

'We're very compatible, you and me, and not just because your ass feels so good when I do this,' he says, pulling me down so I can tumble on top of him, one hand cupping each of my cheeks. He is no longer bookish, not once he's naked; now he's all man, charged up and ready to go. I brush my nipple against his mouth and he takes my gambit, opening wide so I can press seemingly half my breast inside. That is one area where I have an advantage over Serena; I'm a sturdy 36C, while she's a well-proportioned 34B, enhanced by the finest of push-up bras. Rob feasts on each breast and then lets his fingers roam along the crack of my ass before broaching it. 'I want you here,' he says, simple and direct. It's not my usual thing, but the more he plays with my back entrance, the more I want it too.

I know they have lube, I even know exactly where it's tucked away, but I wait for him to offer it to me. There are so many unspoken secrets that I see no need to erase whatever mystery we've managed to conjure thus far. He slips out from beneath me and tells me to stay there, my hair all around me, my right cheek against the pillow, my legs slightly parted, my pussy preening, if a pussy can do such a thing. My hips rise and fall of their own accord, anticipating what he is going to do to me, how he is going to take me in the spot I've never actually been taken in before. I've been kissed there, fondled, and even used a toy, but never have I given a man this ultimate reward, because I've never wanted to. I always thought it would be my husband who I'd give my ass to, but as it turns out, it's someone else's husband, only he feels like mine, right now, at least. We are in a place beyond marriage, a communion where those old-school rules simply don't matter; we aren't so much breaking the rules as making our own, and when he returns and starts licking me there, I surrender.

I've already told my office I may be a little late, that the

161

restaurant where I'm lunching is a bit out of the way and sometimes has poor service. I'm being given the finest service I can imagine, a tongue that is eager and probing, intent on exploring every ridge of my puckered opening. I focus only on opening up for Rob, letting anything else I might know or divine about his anal prowess drop from my mind. This is not about him and her or me and her or anyone other than the two of us. 'Your ass,' he says. Just those two words, seven letters, a promise that he will treat my ass like it is worthy of the finest care, not fragile, but delicate in its way. 'Do you want me here, Carla? Do you want my cock in your ass?'

I turn to look at him, and he is looking back at my face, and that's when I know what it would be like to fall in love with him. I let myself, for just a second, before smiling back, a sultry, sensual smile, not the one I wish I could give him. 'Yes, I do,' I say, my words echoing a marriage vow unintentionally. He slides his slippery fingers inside me – I'm not sure how many, but I'm snug around them – as he slaps his cock against my ass. All of me tightens then, my ass, my pussy, my throat, my fingers around the bedsheets, as I brace myself. He alternates fingers and cock, in and out, in and out, until I scarcely know which is plundering me. He is not the man I'd expected him to be, and I like that he is capable of surprising me. Maybe this is what Serena sees in him; she brings the flamboyance, he brings the spontaneity. Or maybe he just likes the way my ass looks and feels; either way, I'm beyond ready.

I've stopped looking at the clock, stopped looking at anything at all; my eyes are closed, and all my erotic power has now been transferred to the place where our mutual energy is focused. It's like he's plunged a magnet into me, because what I'd once thought only my pussy was capable of I am now feeling in my ass. It's my back channel that is tuning in to the frequency of his pounding cock, his hands pinning my hips down and making me need him when he pulls out for those few almost painful seconds. 'Yes, right there,' I say when he drills into me. I think I'm crying, but they are tears of joy, of discovery, of pure happiness as the tightness seems to take over. When he reaches around me and starts stroking my clit, I almost want to tell him not to, that it's too much, that I will push him out of me, that I can't, but he soothes me by leaning his whole body atop me. He's not a giant of a man, but he is big enough to be warm and comforting as he kisses my back.

Now his cock isn't quite pounding, but claiming, taking, exploring, and my ass, in turn, is getting more and more used to his offering. I know it's about more than just a tight hole, more than just the already illicit nature of our affair. I am giving something to him just as he is giving something to me, a mutual gifting suite. Suddenly I need to see him, and as if he can read my signal, and knows I'm not pushing him away but drawing him close, he pulls out, rolls me over, and repositions himself between my legs. I watch him watching as he enters me, still slick with the lube, and I wrap my legs around his waist.

I look up at him and beam a smile up to him, not a wistful one for all we don't have, but a wide, heart-open one for all that we do. Sometimes you don't get everything all at once, you learn that as a woman maybe you can't have it all, but in that moment, I have everything I want. Well, almost everything, because the longer Rob fucks me, the more I want his come, want it there, so deep inside, so naughty. In truth, I want it everywhere, but inside me is my first priority.

'You want my come, don't you?' he asks, looking into me, practically through me. His eyes have gone a bit glassy, and I wonder what he is thinking about, what this means to him. But I just nod, and he breathes deeply of my hair, then kisses me slowly, his tongue giving mine a chance to press back, just as he's given my hips the chance to rise up toward him and sink down into the bed, my ass the chance to own his cock just as his cock has owned me.

I'm so overcome with emotion I don't know what to say, so I just dig my nails into his back, hard, as if making my mark on his skin will mean something beyond this afternoon, as if I can set new rules by simply exerting the right kind of pressure. I don't know which of our rules I want to keep and which I want to abandon, only that I'm full of more than just his cock, I'm full of something I didn't think you could get from an affair. He whispers nonsense words, or maybe I just don't understand them, but I can tell it's about to happen right before he gives me what I've been craving, and I smile against his cheek as the rush hits me, the warmth of his come like nothing I've felt before. My anus flexes, my body shuddering, and Rob pulls back for a moment to position himself so he can shove his fingers deep into my pussy. I'd thought this wasn't about my pussy, but apparently I was wrong because that is all it takes to have me coming against him, marvelling at how exquisite everything feels, like I've lost a layer of skin and am hyper-sensitive. I come for what feels like five minutes, until I collapse.

I just stare at him, afraid to break the spell. By now it's 3:57 and I have to get going. Neither of us seems to know what to say, so I let him drag me to the bathroom where he tenderly washes my most intimate parts with warm washcloths and helps me get dressed before pressing me into a cab. We don't speak of next time, not yet.

The next time I see Serena, she tells me she has a surprise for me. 'I want your ass,' she says with her usual wicked grin. For a terrifying moment I'm afraid she's cottoned on to me and Rob, that our secret, special time has just become another risqué anecdote for them to share. But then she shows me a new dildo she's sporting, one slightly smaller than Rob's cock, one that suits her perfectly. And while before I might have hesitated to let her back there, now when I get on all fours and let her enter me, I get the thrill of her thrusts and the echo of Rob's at the same time, and that is a secret I don't have to share with anyone.

Real
by Jaye Raymee

She was beautiful. Long, golden-blonde hair with honey highlights; teeth that, in their slight crookedness, gave her face a special character; a body that was curvy and plump in all the right places. He had loved running his hands through her hair and his mouth along her skin, from her toes to her neck and back down, until she shivered and laughingly told him, no, *begged* him to stop or to finish her off.

That was before the booze and the pills and the extra hundred pounds on her small frame had built a barrier between them that he couldn't breach no matter how hard he tried. So he did what millions of men through the ages had done: he gave up.

The strange thing about giving up, he thought, watching the redhead who had just entered the bar, is that once you've done so, everything becomes possible. It's as if all the energy you were expending on trying to reach that one goal instead lights up the universe and exposes a wealth of possibility and potential.

And it really hadn't been cheating, he figured.

Especially that first time, which had started in this same bar. It was so damned *electric*, to kiss another woman after ten years of the same lips in the same patterns. The girl from the office had even looked like his wife, or at least as they had looked when they first met. Same honey-gold highlights, same slightly plump frame, same slightly demure attitude. He had been astonished when he felt her knee brush up against his leg during an after-work happy hour. To ensure that he knew it wasn't an accident, she pressed more insistently against him until he moved his hand down to lightly touch her nylon-clad thigh. Her own hand had caught and held his below the level of the table, and her fingers had lightly caressed the back of his palm. He felt like a kid in a movie theatre, unable to pay attention to what was going on around him because what was important, what was real, was happening in the dark, out of sight.

And later, when he'd walked her to her car, she had turned to him and nearly thrown herself at him. She had parked in a dark corner, and they were mostly safe from prying eyes, but it was still definitely outside, and exposed to anybody who might pass by. That made it even more exciting. She flung her arms and legs around him, and he lifted her up onto the edge of some random piece of urban decoration (a planter? The back of a bench?). They made out like teenagers, all sloppy kisses and clumsy, over-the-clothes fumbling. Like a teenager, she wouldn't let him move his hand under her shirt to touch her breasts, but she ground herself against him and he slid one hand between her legs where he could feel her wetness soaking through her clothes as she moved faster and faster against him. She held his head to her chest, and he could her heart speeding up as she approached her climax. Her breath was hot in his ears as she came, sounding almost as if she was in pain as she shuddered and groaned against him. He listened as her breathing calmed, and she gave a final sigh and untangled her hand from his hair and her legs from around him.

He didn't know what to expect, after, but on some level he thought there would be some reciprocity. Instead, she gave him a long, lingering kiss and then got unsteadily into the driver's seat and left. He had gone home alone, all the alcohol burned out of his system by the frustrated endorphins floating around in his brain waiting for release, like frat boys who'd showed up at a prayer meeting instead of a kegger. When he got home, his wife lay in a gin-and-Valium haze watching videos of *Beverly Hills 90210*.

He went to bed alone, figuring that come Monday he'd see if there was a chance for another get-together with the girl. Maybe something they'd both enjoy, this time. She had certainly seemed into it tonight, even if she'd taken off before he'd had a chance to get his own back.

But, back in the office the next week, she'd barely met his eyes, and she'd brushed off any hints about meeting for a drink or maybe dinner. His probes were met with the universal, 'Sure, maybe, but I'm pretty busy,' that every smart man knows means *no*.

And the next one, come on, that *certainly* wasn't cheating.

While away at a conference, he had noticed a skinny, slightly foreign-looking woman with short black hair who was eyeing him during a particularly boring panel discussion about a tri-lateral tax treaty and its implications for expatriate wage earners. As fellow torture victims in that situation often do, they had kept each other amused from a distance by pantomiming their boredom, telegraphing signals that meant "Kill me now" and "Wrap it up, already!" until they were both nearly laughing out loud in their seats. When he had raised his hand and made a drinking gesture just before the interminable droning ended, the woman looked at her watch and nodded, holding up five fingers and pointing at the hotel lounge area just outside the meeting room door. He lost her in the crowd as they all escaped, and he had no idea if she meant she only had five minutes or she'd be along in five minutes. Either way, the price of a drink was a small one to pay for keeping him amused, and he waited for her to show up in the bar.

She made it there inside the five minutes, and had more than that to spare. They spent the first few drinks talking about the conference, the next few comparing career stories, and somewhere between talking about their families and making the smart choice to call it a night and head to their respective rooms, he decided it would be fun to see what would happen if he made a pass at her. It would be almost more for laughs than anything else; he'd do nearly anything to alleviate the boredom of two more days of lectures. It had been so long since he'd made a move on a woman that he almost didn't know how to start. Fortunately, one more shot of Patrón Silver made him bold enough to say, 'You know, they're about to close this place down, but my minibar is part of my expense account, and I make a mean minibar margarita.' The booze had obviously affected her too, because, in spite of the cheap line, she didn't hesitate.

She slapped her hand on the table, a little too loudly and said in a stage whisper, 'Sounds great! I *drink* a mean minibar margarita!'

Back in his room, part of him wondered if he'd be able to do much with so much alcohol on board, and part of him wondered if he'd actually go through with it in any case, but he wasted no time in getting the drinks ready.

The woman's slightly olive complexion was accented by the deep black of her hair, and in the dim light of his room she took on an even more exotic look, like something out of a Merchant Ivory film. When he handed her the drink, he noticed something he hadn't before: a sizeable diamond on her finger, and another band above it, this one with five diamonds set in it. Five years married, he thought, hazily. He'd bought his wife a similar ring, back before he'd given up, back when he could never have imagined himself in a dark hotel room with another woman.

A woman who was now sitting on his bed, having slipped off her shoes in a gesture of startling intimacy, and had curled her legs up underneath herself like a cat.

He sat down next to her, and tentatively reached out one hand to touch hers. She responded by raising his hand to her lips and lightly kissing his knuckles, one after the other. He slipped his arm around her, and they laid back together on the king-sized bed in a fog of tequila and her perfume, his lips on hers, his hands reaching down to her trim waist, her slim thighs parting slightly at his touch.

She kissed him back just as passionately, and then guided his mouth to her breast, where he could feel her stiffening through the cloth as the heat from his mouth warmed the sensitive skin of her nipples. He smoothly unbuttoned her blouse and freed her eager nipple from the black lace push-up bra she wore underneath, tasting both her skin and the lace that still clung to it. She moaned as he teased her into even greater alertness, and he saw her other hand move to the breast that that was still trapped. She lifted it out of its cup, and kneaded it softly in time to his suckling.

He slid one hand between her legs, up inside the narrow skirt she was still wearing. Underneath, he discovered that she was wearing garters, and he was able to slide his hand across the bare skin of her thighs as she opened more fully to his touch. She sighed as his fingers found her slick tunnel, and he slipped inside her, his thumb finding and stroking the pulsing button of flesh above her entrance. He had barely touched it when her body went rigid, so stiff he was almost startled, but the squeeze of pressure around his fingers and the rush of wetness told him that she had come, and come hard.

For a skinny thing, she was strong, and he found himself being rolled over on his back before he quite realised what was happening. She straddled him, rubbing his straining organ with her own mound, making him think he would lose it while still fully dressed. Another wave passed through her, and she collapsed onto his chest, breathing hard as she recovered.

He felt his own shirt being unbuttoned, and a trail of kisses like a line of fire going down his chest, past his navel, and without even seeming to try, she had his belt off and his pants pulled down. His cock sprang to attention and was enveloped in her soft grip. He let out a groan, and, taking that for encouragement, the woman continued her trail of kisses from his stomach to the top of his shaft, then with tongue and teeth made her way to the sensitive head.

She took him into her mouth, shallowly at first and then he was all the way inside her, her tongue rolling against him like a serpent made out of silk and oil. He'd never been deep-throated before, but now felt his cock being drawn into her throat and stroked there by her tongue and muscles. She was doing something with her thumb at the underside of his shaft, putting pressure on some sensitive point, his back arched with sudden abandon, coming like he hadn't done in years, pumping great spurts into the woman's mouth, which kept working him until he finally subsided, and she drew her head back, caressing his softening length even as she let it slip from her mouth with agonising slowness.

He could barely move, and even the slight stir of her breath across his spent member made him twitch and nearly cry out. He heard a throaty chuckle of satisfaction as she moved up and laid her head on the pillow beside him, her hand trailing along his chest.

Ridiculous as it was, the strains of the *Macarena* burst out from somewhere nearby. He felt the woman sit up beside him.

'Shit,' she said, 'It's my kids.' He felt her move off the bed toward her purse. Her cell phone! She grabbed it and disappeared into the bathroom with it.

Far from offended, he wondered what he would do it his phone rang just now. It would only ever be his wife, checking in with him before heading home from a girls-night with a bunch of other boozing wives at their club. She'd give him a slurred good night and pop another sleeping pill once she was home, and then fall asleep on the couch since he wasn't there to make her get up and get into a real bed. Would he answer it? Would it matter? He realised that he would answer it, and that it did matter. As

172

crappy as things had been for the past several years, he was not going to screw with what few traditions they had left.

The woman came out of the bathroom, clicking the phone shut as she walked over to him. Her shirt was still in disarray, but she had fixed her bra and he could tell from her body language that the night was over.

It was her kids, she explained, some problem at home that she had to take care of. She was so sorry that she had to go, but maybe a drink tomorrow night? Maybe dinner? She bustled about, buttoning her top, shrugging into her coat, grabbing her purse. He could barely follow her with his eyes, as he felt a post-coitus torpor spread from his groin out to his arms and legs. She had to go, it had been a great evening, she'd see him tomorrow?

She didn't show up to the rest of the conference. When he asked casually about her, he was told there had been some family emergency that had popped up. He didn't know her last name, just her first name, from the name badge provided by the conference organisers. He knew it wouldn't matter even if he did know it. She was gone, back to her world, to her family, and tomorrow night he'd be doing the same, going back to his life too.

Even the hooker hadn't really been cheating, he figured, his attention returning to the bar he was sitting in. The redhead across the bar was making her way over to him now, and taking the empty seat next to him. He signalled the bartender to get her a drink, any drink at all.

The hooker had been more like a bucket-list thing, not really infidelity. It was an experience, something to cross off before he died. "Pay for sex" was hard to do, if you were married and disinclined to cheat. But he'd been in Amsterdam with a client, and what the hell, if smoking pot were wasn't illegal here, then a quickie behind red curtains with a woman who got paid up front wasn't really an affair.

The only truly satisfying part of the experience was the warm cloth she'd used to bathe his cock and scrotum with

173

before slipping on the condom, and again after he'd finished. He'd picked the hooker based on the size of her boobs, and had been wondering what it would be like to squeeze tits that big. Even that had been a bust; she'd slapped his hands away as he'd been about to touch them, and then she had clinically thrust away at him until he was done. She spent the whole time looking at some point over his shoulder, at some mystery vision of her own imagining. He had felt about as fulfilled as the sad little latex tube that she'd tied off and tossed into a wicker basket with its abandoned fellows.

No, he thought, glancing again at the redhead who was regarding him with frank appraisal in the mirror on the bar, it didn't count. None of it had mattered.

Later, back at the redhead's apartment, she placed a tentative hand in his as they walked into the bedroom. He squeezed it firmly, and her arms went around him, his around her. Her breasts, which were the first thing that had attracted him to her when they first met, were pale and had a sprinkling of freckles across their tops. He kissed the constellation there, and more, her nipples hard and long as he kept one wet and captive in his mouth while the other was teased by her hand over his, her breathing speeding up in time with the increasing pace and pressure she was squeezed with.

When she straddled him, her breasts hung low and inviting. She held his head to their sweetly pillowing softness, her hands tangling gently in his hair. He didn't remember getting naked, but they both were, and his hands went down to her hips, then her thighs, his thumbs slowly the sensitive hollow where they met.

His cock was pressed almost painfully against his stomach as she stroked it with her nether lips, sliding back and forth on top of his, moving faster as he kept his thumbs moving against her throbbing pearl. She ground against him, her own head thrown back, and he knew that her orgasm was close as both her hands gripped his head tighter and she pushed her tit almost savagely into him mouth. He had learned her body over the past months, as his wife had sunk lower and lower into whatever hell her inner demons drove her to, but none of that had counted, it wasn't real.

Her pale skin was shimmering and slick with sweat now, and he could taste the salt on her breasts. Her first orgasm made her cry out and squeeze his head almost painfully into her bosom.

She was different somehow from the people he'd been around for so long, more alive in some way. In spite of himself, he'd grown more than fond of her, learning more about her, and letting her know more about him.

She began to kiss her way down his body, in a ritual that they had developed over the time they'd been together, a series of stolen evenings and afternoons spent in illicit discovery. As her hand reached to stroke him, to put him between those wonderful breasts and bring him to his own release, he stopped her, and subtly shifted their positions.

She was still astride him, but now he held himself just at the entrance to her dripping sheath. Looking into her eyes, he rubbed his glans around her swollen vulva, and enjoyed the faint gasp she gave as he slowly slid the tip up and down the length of her labia.

He had learned this body so well in such a short time, but he saw the question in her eyes – they had never done *this*, before, so much else but never this final connection.

He drew in a deep breath, and with a slight pressure on her hips, slowly drove her down on to his hard length until he was buried entirely in her flesh. She moved slightly, as they rocked together, but she kept her eyes open and on his as their tempo grew more and more frantic. He was almost lost, looking into those twin emerald depths, and he felt like their breaths were coming from the same set of lungs as they moved faster and faster, his cock deep inside her and every inch of her tight tunnel squeezing him in the same rhythm as

175

their breath.

They only lost eye contact at the very end, when he pulled her into a tight embrace and, with a final thrust, she screamed his name and shuddered explosively, and he poured himself into her, his seed spilling deep into her being, his sudden, '*I love you,*' blending with hers as they swayed and shook together. He knew this was different. He knew that this counted, that the difference was ... this was real.

Afterward, lying quietly but still unable to catch their breath, neither of them even moved when his phone rang.

Ready or Not, Here I Come
by Lynn Lake

Tess Jansen just had to get laid. Before the summer was over, and she had to buckle down to the drudgery of community college in the fall. She'd turned 18 in April, and now she was so ripe and juicy, ready and willing, that she could hardly slip her little white shorty-shorts on without coming. She was a grown-up girl with grown-up needs, just aching to be popped.

Only problem was, Tess's boyfriend, Mike "The Bike" Handler, didn't seem to understand her need. Didn't get it. Either too lazy, or scared, or wrapped up in busting moves on his skateboard and BMX to bust the cherry of his brimming girlfriend.

Tess had been sending out urgent smoke signals since grad – rubbing up against the guy (in an effort to kindle a fire), whispering naughty nothings in his ear (and out the other, apparently), playing some of her father's porn stash DVDs whenever Mike came over to freeload the Xtreme Sports channel. But the guy was deaf and dumb to her mature, girly desires. And Tess Jansen was still too much of a lady to just reach out and grab his hose and stick it right in her burning hole.

'Rub some lotion on my back, Mike?' she cooed.

She was stretched out on her tummy on an air mattress next to her parents' swimming pool. Her blonde hair was braided into pigtails that lay on her sun-browned shoulders

177

like spun wheat, her curvy, glistening, baby-fat body exploding out of a teensy, pink string bikini.

Tess's parents were away at marriage counselling for the afternoon, and lying under the glaring sun, next to the sparkling water, eyeing her boyfriend's wiry physique displayed in just a pair of knee-length biker shorts, had turned the girl's teen bod and brain molten with desire. Her C-cup titties tingled, her kitten-pink nipples so hard they were puncturing holes in the plastic air mattress, her bikini-shaved cunny squishy with way more than just pool water. All it would take was Mike's oversized hands on her electrified skin and she'd burst like a water balloon.

'Huh? What?' the guy mumbled, picking at a scab on his knee. Then he pricked up his ears, cocked his head to one side. Tess thought he was hearing the clarion call of her raging hormones, the humming of her sizzling body. But she was sadly mistaken.

'Hey, sounds like Pipe-Squeak,' Mike said, rising to his feet at the sound of someone banging a skateboard down on the street out front, the grinding of ball-bearinged wheels on gritty pavement.

Tess pushed up on to her elbows and popped a spaghetti strap off her shoulder. 'Won't you rub some –'

'Oh, man! Wipe-out!' Mike yelped, grinning at the sound of his buddy crashing and cursing. 'Sweet!' He flipped his board up off the grass and trotted around the side of the house. Leaving his girlfriend all by her lonesome.

She pounded the air mattress with her little fists, tears of despair flooding her big, blue eyes.

'I've got your back covered, Tess,' someone said, then laughed.

Tess twisted her head around, wiping her face as she spotted Bernie Morris, the next-door neighbour, peering at her from over the cedar fence that separated the two properties. 'Oh ... hi, Mr Morris,' she groaned. 'How you doin'?'

'Doin' better all the time,' the man replied, his black eyes flashing with the searing image of all that gleaming, brown, girlish flesh on display. 'Mind if I come over?'

'No ... come if you want,' Tess muttered, before burying her face in the mattress.

Bernie worked at the same plant as Tess's father, but in a different department. In exchange for a ride to work every day, he had free access to the pool whenever he wanted.

'Water sure looks tempting,' he commented, after racing through his backyard, down the back lane, and through the rear gate in his neighbour's fence. He wasn't admiring the cool, crystal-clear waters of the swimming pool as he struggled to get his breath back, and couldn't, however. He was admiring something even more tempting: the burgeoning, breathtaking figure of his neighbour's daughter up-close, coveting every shining, sun-dappled inch of her smooth, ultra-hot bod.

'Dive right in, Mr Morris,' Tess said, not turning her head to notice the hard-on bulging the front of the forty-year-old's white Dockers. 'I'm not in the mood.'

'Please, call me Bernie,' he responded. He licked his lips and slicked back his jet-black hair with a shaking hand, striding rapidly around the pool, eyes and dick bedazzled by the sunny blonde's mounded, palm-filling butt cheeks. He could almost feel her heated, pliant flesh, as he rubbed suntan lotion, among other things, into her.

He was so wrapped up in his shamefully sexy thoughts, in fact, that he failed to notice the pool skimmer lying by the side of the dunk tank. He tripped over the handle, then caught his foot in the netting. He stumbled to the edge of the pool, flapping his flippers like an overgrown penguin in a futile effort to regain his balance. He took a header into the deep end.

Tess looked around at the sound of the splash. Then she giggled behind her hand as she watched her neighbour flail around in the water in all of his clothing.

But when he went under for the third time, it finally dawned on the teenager that the man actually had troubles of his own. She rolled off the air mattress and dove into the water, splitting the surface cleanly (she'd been on the swim team in high school, after all). She popped up right in front of the panicked man, grabbed on to his belt, and quickly towed him into shallower waters.

'Th-th-thanks!' Bernie blubbered. 'Th-thanks a lot!'

Even as he was fighting to get water out of his lungs and air into them, he was staring at the teenie's bobbing breasts, feeling the girl's hot little hand pressing against his stomach where she gripped him, her knuckles brushing the swollen cap of his erection. She was a vision of mermaid-in-training loveliness in front of him, water dripping off her golden hair and bronzed shoulders, streaming down into the warm, brown hollow of her cleavage. Her chest buoys heaved up and down, the wet imprint of her rigid nipples providing the salty exclamation points on a mouthwatering body that siren-songed, 'Take me! Please, take me!'

He already had his left arm wrapped around her shoulders, to steady himself, and now he drew her closer, pressing her soft body against his hard need. He ground his iron lung into her flat tummy, staring down into her liquid eyes.

'Uh, no need to ... thank me, Mr ... Bernie,' Tess said, the pulsing in her own body suddenly flaring up stronger than ever now.

'But I insist,' the man replied, knowing the girl needed, wanted the full extent of his thanks.

He fished his hands down into the water and caught on to her buoyant butt cheeks, cradling and cupping, squeezing the thick, peachy flesh. Then he bent his head down and pressed his mouth against Tess's warm, wet mouth. Taking hold of the steamy virgin with his hands and his lips.

Tess didn't know how to react. This guy feeling up her bottom, kissing her right on the lips like men weren't supposed to kiss girls, was old enough to be her father's friend. But still ... was she actually feeling the hornies like she felt with Mike all the time? Could the tingling in her cunny be wrong?

She squirmed her hand all the way into Bernie's pants, grabbing on to the man's log.

'Yes, Tess!' he groaned, pulling his mouth away, but not his hands. 'That's the way, baby.' He was a sorry sight in his soaked Hawaiian shirt and mussed-up hair, but with a teen hottie gripping and tugging on his dong, her butt mounds filling his grasping hands, he felt anything but sorry.

He pulled the string on Tess's bikini, yanking the skimpy swimsuit bottom away from her body. Then he fumbled his zipper and belt open and shoved his pants and Jockeys down, so that they were both bare south of the equator, below the waterline. He swam his fingers over the girl's smouldering pussy.

'Mmmm!' Tess moaned. She shivered with delight, despite the heat, because of the heat, the man's experienced fingers feeling so very fine riffling through her bed of fur, tickling her swollen, sensitive lips.

Bernie gently stroked Tess's kitty, feeling the girl shudder against him, her hand jerk on his pulsating cock. He rubbed harder, faster, and she really pulled on his prick, her soft, warm hand flying up and down the raging length of his dong beneath the water.

The superheated air went stiflingly breathless, the sun beating down, the only sounds the two lover's muted moans and whimpers, the water washing against their quivering bodies masking the turmoil below. Bernie drove his tongue into Tess's open mouth, up against her tongue, urgently buffing the girl's slit as she pumped him the handie of his life.

Tess sucked on the man's thrashing tongue, her body and face flushing to fever pitch with the fervour of his fingers on her electrified cun, her brimming clitty. She recklessly pulled on his meat-organ – like she wasn't doing such a dirty thing for the very first time – jolted by lightning bolts of joy that burst from her finger-scrubbed muff and shimmered all through her. She swelled with erotic energy, then exploded.

'Mike ... Mr Morris ... Bernie!' she wailed, trembling out of control, churning up the water with wet and wild orgasm.

'Tess, baby!' Bernie yelled back, his cock and body spasming in her jacking hand.

He sunk his fingers into her pussy and felt the deeper heat of her juices squirting out into the water as she jerked waterlogged ropes of semen out of his jumping dick, draining him body and soul.

Tess became even more determined to get her boyfriend to pop her cherry. If it could feel so gooey good at the hand of an old man, just imagine what being pricked by a boy her own age would feel like. Full-on fabulous, she bet.

So she made arrangements for Mike and herself to spend the entire weekend camping all by themselves. Her father wasn't doing any handsprings over the idea, while her mother just sighed and looked wistful. But Tess explained that they'd be staying at George Adamas' campground – the nephew of another friend of her dad's – and sleeping in separate tents, of course.

With those feeble assurances that his blushing virgin daughter would be both safe and sound, Tess's father patted her on the head and gave his OK, little realising what a hot-blooded woman lay beneath the innocent braids and braces. Fathers are usually the last to know.

'Isn't it super-beautiful?' Tess enthused, skidding to a stop on a rocky outcropping that overlooked a bright, blue lake below. After mountain biking for a half-hour straight, she and Mike were now buried deep in the countryside, surrounded by emerald green forest, sun-heated rock, and sparkling water on all sides.

Mike pinched down a nostril, blew out the other. 'Yeah ... whatever,' he mumbled, more interested in checking out the chain on his BMX than the scenery.

Tess gazed at the young man in the hip-hop shorts and *Jackass* T-shirt, her big, blue eyes flooding with want, her boisterous body surging with a heat more than weather and exercise related. She was clad in just a pink tank-top and a pair of white shorty-shorts, her ripened boobies just about falling out of the skimpy top, the tangy scent of her girly juices strong in the hot, still air. Goosebumps prickled her bare, blonde-dusted arms and legs, her buds sproinging so hard she could barely resist pushing them up and sucking on them herself.

She fell off her bike, then scrambled to her feet, swaying slightly, the blood rushing in between her legs. This was it. This had to be it.

She clutched her one true love's hand and pulled him off his bike. Then dragged him over to the lone picnic table that stood next to a brick barbecue pit overlooking the lake. Staring him meaningfully in the eye, she bunny-hopped butt-backwards up onto the picnic table, then lay back on the weathered slats, spreading her arms and legs. Offering herself up like a Sunday picnic buffet, a virgin sacrifice. She breathed, 'Take –'

'Hey, dude! Spinnin' your wheels, or what!?' someone yelled from the trail.

Mike spun around, spotted his buddy, Spokes-man.

'Beat you back to the campground, dude!' Spokes-man shouted.

Mike raced back to his BMX and took up the challenge, peddling his skinny ass off down the hard-packed trail after his buddy. Leaving forlorn, forgotten Tess sprawled out on the picnic table. She stared up into the sun, heartfelt tears rolling down her chubby cheeks, breasts bouncing spasmodically in rhythm to her plaintive sobs.

183

'You look good 'nuff to eat, Tess,' George Adamas's uncle, Nick, remarked, stepping out of the brush. He was the spitting image of his nephew, only twenty years older, short and stocky, with curly, grey hair and lively brown eyes. He'd been taking a bathroom break after cleaning out the brickwork barbecue, but now he saw something that could really get a fire going. He hustled over to the table full of Tess.

She raised her head, the pink ribbons on the ends of her braids glinting in the sun. 'Oh, hi, Mr A – senior,' she pouted. 'I was just, um, you know, admiring the scenery.'

'Me too.' Nick grinned, getting up right next to the picnic table, in between Tess's dangling legs. He licked a pair of parched lips, then set his hairy, sweaty hands down on the girl's plump thighs.

'Uh, Mr –'

'Yup, good 'nuff to eat.' He swallowed hard, kneading Tess's thighs. Then he dipped his head down and licked the wet stain on the front of the girl's shorts.

'Oooh!' Tess squealed. The man's tongue on her soft spot jolted her, juiced her up again.

Nick quickly unzipped and popped the teen's shorts open, pulled the damp, hanky-sized garment off Tess's bum and partway down her legs. Exposing puffy, pink lips glistening with moisture, blonde fur matted with liquid lust. Nick stuck out his tongue and dove right into the girl's gooey centre.

'Ohmigod!' Tess yelped, shuddering with the impact of wet tongue on bare slitty.

Nick wedged his tongue deep into her pie, tasting her honey-sweet juices, exploring her meaty softness. He licked Tess's kitty, running his tongue all the way up from her puckered bumhole to the top of her springy furline. Over and over, paying special attention to the teenie's swelled-up button.

Tess clawed at the man's curls, shaking all over, lit up

like a July 4th firecracker with the wet, wonderful sensation of a man's beaded tongue dragging over her super-sensitive slit. It only took a mouthful of long, hard tongue-strokes before she was ready to spill her joy. Which was exactly when Nick pulled his head back.

He looked at the girl staring desperately at him, his lips slick with her slime, his eyes twinkling. 'You hungry too, Tess?'

She had no idea what he was talking about. Until he dropped his baggy pants and striped shorts and climbed up on the picnic table with her, straddling her head, lowering his twitching slab of a cock down into her face.

Tess gazed up at the man's towering dong. Then she parted her petulant lips and sucked mushroomed cockhead into her warm, wet mouth. Nick grunted, jerked, as Tess eagerly tugged on his hood, sucking like she'd seen a slut in one of her father's pornos suck.

She earnestly gulped more and more of Nick's vein-ridged dong. Then pulled back, then mouthed him halfway down again. She started rocking her head back and forth, wet-vaccing the man's pulsing hammer.

'Fuck!' Nick groaned, his knees shaking and sweat pouring off his reddened face, pattering down onto the wood.

Tess took him at his word. 'Yes, please,' she gasped from around his throbber.

'Huh? Oh.' He'd seen that misty look in a girl's eyes before.

He gingerly kneed his way back off the table, off Tess, his dick bobbing wet and raw every inch of the way. And as he planted his work boots back down on the ground again, Tess kicked her shorts away and squirmed her legs wide open, offering her steaming cooch up on a heated wooden platter.

Nick grabbed and shouldered the girl's legs, gripped his enraged prong and speared it into her oiled opening. Tess screamed, not from any real pain, but from the imagined pain. The first time *was* supposed to hurt, wasn't it?

But it didn't. It felt wonderful – a dizzy, full-up feeling that was both strangely delicious and oh-so-adult. She popped her eyes open and stared at the intersection of the old man and herself. His prick was totally buried inside her womanhood, hairy balls to the pink pussy-walls. She beamed, wishing only vaguely that her boyfriend was there to experience it, and her, for the very first time.

Nick dug his dirty fingernails into Tess's damp thighs and churned his hips, sawing away at the girl with his cock. She was tight, but wickedly juicy, her slick, elastic pussy lips milking his dong as he drove it home. Tess yanked up her tank and grabbed on to her bare titties, squeezing the shuddering puddings, rolling her engorged nipples.

Nick pumped faster, huffing and puffing, pounding Tess's sucking twat, his stout body splashing against her rippling bum cheeks. Tess moaned and pulled harder on her nubbins, rocking back and forth in rhythm to Nick's frantic thrusting.

They went into meltdown under the blazing sun, Nick bucking, pouring white-hot sperm deep into the writhing girl; Tess screaming, twisting her head from side-to-side, pigtails flying, wild with her first-ever full-on orgasm. Her heated gush coated Nick's jerking cock, both of them blown away by ecstasy.

Even though her boyfriend, Mike, had proven to be a total romantic klutz and dud lover, Tess still adored the boy with all of her heart. So long as there was an older, more experienced man around to take care of her seething sexual needs, that was.

The Game
by Daniel Savage

The man checked in at the hotel reception just as he had a hundred times before. He knew the routine better than the counter staff so had no difficulty in letting his attention drift to the woman who had arrived just behind him.

She was dressed in a black business suit, high heels, stockings (he was almost sure), a white blouse barely restraining her perfectly full breasts, and spectacles. She was the personification of his ultimate fantasy and he could not help but let his eyes linger too long to avoid impropriety.

She noticed his gaze and he knew it. Wrenching himself back to the clerk he accepted the room key and made off. He knew he would be able to snatch another full-body glance when he reached the footwell of the stairs and he made no mistake.

Probably late thirties, she was still slim, although her curves simply accentuated a femininity which seemed to dominate her immediate environment. Her tight skirt surrounded an exquisite bottom, her legs were shapely with that womanly definition which is always enhanced by heels and her breasts were clear in their outline as she turned sideways. It was all he could do to wrest his eyes away. Then he was gone. And so was she.

On reaching his room he decided not to masturbate there and then. He was tired from the day's travails and knew his erection would be much stronger in the morning, as would his orgasm. The woman had provided the most enticing new material and she deserved at least a few hours' cogitation to build the right mental picture of how best to enjoy her.

The fantasy was not long in filling his mind as he lay on the bed and clicked on the TV. It was one he had worked on many times during his long, lonely hours in hotel rooms such as this.

Was it possible, he thought, for two people to reach new heights of sexual frisson without ever making physical contact with each other? To engage in a full blown sexual interchange which possessed everything except the actual touch and feel? He thought it was, and he had rehearsed the steps as to how it might happen a thousand times.

He would find himself chatting to an intriguing lady in a hotel where they were both staying. The conversation would somehow get around to sex and each other's preferences and they would talk graphically and explicitly about their experiences. Despite the intense, mutual arousal both would agree it could go no further as both are married.

Instead, he would suggest they play a game in which the sexual, conversational theme continued but which had each of them in a dominant and submissive role, depending on who was taking the lead.

The rules were simple. Each could ask the other to do or discuss anything and the other, as the submissive, must agree. If the submissive felt unable to agree then the game would immediately be over.

They would pass the sexual charge to each other intermittently as new instructions and questions popped into their heads. But it would always be clear as to who was sub, who was dom and when the switch had been made.

Neither would know how explicit the role play would become. Neither would know how far she or he wanted to go, or when the other would call a halt. That was the attraction, the uncertainty, the danger and the excitement.

The only other rule of course; no physical contact must

take place between the two of them and all questions, however personal, must be answered honestly.

The man thought he knew the logical direction the game should take. But of course, he didn't know the woman or how she would react.

Thirty minutes later, back in the bar which adjoined reception, he ordered his complimentary beer. As he swivelled on his stool to take in the room, the woman appeared and stood just a couple of yards away, still in her business attire. He experienced one of those confused moments between surprise and opportunity and tried to look unaffected by her presence.

She too took her beer and enquired about food. The bartender pushed a menu into her hand and she began to browse.

The man watched intently, not quite believing his luck as his eyes got a second feast of this acutely feminine and captivating creature.

'Not much of a choice, is there?' she said, smiling in his direction.

Heart springing out of his chest, he managed to mumble some inane response before gathering himself and offering, 'Actually I've eaten in here a few times and it's not that bad. Is there nothing on there that you fancy?'

'Oh, I suppose so,' she answered. 'But I get so tired of hotel food, don't you?'

This now counted as a proper conversation and the man's adrenaline was racing. She was actually talking to him and seemed in no hurry to terminate the pleasantries.

'I know what you mean. That's why I often don't bother. I never turn a drink down, though,' he said, raising his glass and trying to look collected.

'You not eating tonight?' she enquired.

'Doubt it. May be later but I'm in no rush,' he said.

'No, I don't suppose there is,' she said, lowering the

menu and pushing it away.

It was now she would either drink up, start fiddling with her mobile, return to her room or just walk off and sit out of sight, indicating that the conversation was over. Incredibly, she did none of these things.

'You know this place well then?' she asked, popping herself on a stool and resting one elbow on the bar.

The man really had to engage his brain now. This dialogue was going on to a whole new level and he didn't want to sound anything but calm and controlled.

He glanced at her wedding finger before answering. Married, obviously, but he wasn't going to let that spoil any fun. So was he, for that matter.

'Yes, I stay here at least once a week. It's so handy and really quite comfortable.'

There followed a good 20 minutes of easy conversation, mainly about work and careers. There was the odd reference to families but neither party particularly wanted to pry. When glasses were empty, the man assumed once again that this would be the end of the interlude.

He asked, more out of courtesy than expectation, if she would like another drink.

'Why not?' came the reply, with the very faintest hint of a mischievous smile. Whatever she was doing, she was doing it so well!

As they had talked the man had undressed her several times in his mind's eye. It was becoming increasingly difficult to avoid her cleavage and when she crossed and re-crossed her legs on the bar stool, her skirt rode enticingly higher each time.

Quite how the conversation shifted, he didn't know. But when it came it was unmissable.

'It's a good job we are both away from home,' she said. 'I'll bet we look like classic affair material sitting here chatting like this.'

'You think so? I can't see that anyone's taking any

notice, and anyway we haven't done anything to raise any eyebrows, have we?' he said.

She smiled that barely noticeable smile once again and asked, 'You work away from home all the time, have you ever been tempted?'

'Frequently,' he answered honestly. 'You?'

'Can't be avoided, can it, really?' she said. 'So much opportunity and who would ever know? But so far I've managed to behave.'

'So far?' he asked.

'It could happen but I don't like the thought of being unfaithful,' she explained.

The man paused. He knew that a million-to-one chance had landed in his lap and he knew he could not pass it up. Whatever the response, he had to ask the question. If the evening ended there and then, it was already worth it.

'What if there was a way to have the most incredible sexual experience without ever making physical contact with the other person. Could you live with that?' he asked, aware that his voice was wavering slightly.

'Not sure what you mean,' she said, rather sweetly.

'It's simple. We play a game. We retire to a bedroom and there we talk freely about our sexual preferences and experiences, all questions to be answered honestly and explicitly. But at any time either of us can ask the other to do something,' he explained.

'Such as?' she inquired.

'Well, you might be speaking and I might ask you to undo a button of your blouse,' he said.

'Just one?'

'The next time I asked it might be two. Or I might ask you to do something else. If there is something that I ask that you feel you cannot do then that ends the game. And of course you can ask me the same and I must do it.'

'What like?' she asked, showing an increasing interest in the idea.

191

'You might ask me if I had an erection and, if so, to describe it to you.'

'Mmmm,' she pondered. 'Yes, I suppose I could do that.'

'The only rule is that we cannot touch. There must be no physical contact whatsoever,' the man went on. 'The fun is in the fact that neither of us knows when or how the game will end.'

The woman paused for what seemed like an eternity. The man thought he might have misjudged the whole moment. But something told him to go for the close.

'It's my fantasy,' he said. 'I've never actually played the game with anyone. We could try and see where it goes.'

The pause continued. Then that imperceptible smile returned and the woman nodded slowly.

'I'm intrigued,' she said. 'Let's begin.'

Trying desperately hard to control his elation, the man assumed the dominant role. After all, this was his idea and he knew he would have to lead for a little while.

'Describe your last orgasm to me,' he said very directly, thus setting the tone and reasserting his position of interrogator. He wouldn't have been surprised if the woman had been flustered straight away and ended the game there and then. But she took the question completely in her stride.

'It was this morning actually,' she said. 'I was staying in another hotel and awoke early. I felt horny so started playing with myself under the duvet. I was soon very wet and I came quite quickly,' she added almost matter-of-factly. 'That's the beauty of DIY, don't you think? You know which buttons to press!'

'Did you fantasise about anyone or anything?' the man asked.

'I did allow a brief moment of reflection about one of my work colleagues to enter the proceedings,' she said.

'You find him attractive?'

'Very much so. He is much younger than me and I simply can't stop myself wanting to teach him a few things,' she smiled.

'Such as?'

'I want to know if he has the experience to make love to me properly or if he just wants to fuck me. If it's the latter, then he has much to learn.'

This was going exactly to plan and as the woman talked, the man felt his cock begin to stiffen, not to full erection, but enough to signal the first pulse of precome down the shaft and into his pants.

'Were you thinking of him when you came this morning?'

'Not at the precise moment,' she said. 'I just wanted to enjoy my orgasm so I concentrated on my clit in a way that only I know.

'Are you getting hard?' she asked out of the blue. Her timing was perfect. She had switched roles without being prompted and her question was exactly in keeping with how the game should be played.

'Yes I am,' the man answered honestly, realising that he had now been made the submissive. God, she was good!

It was the woman who issued the first command.

'I want you to swivel on the stool so that I get a full view of your crotch,' she said firmly. 'Then I want you to open your legs to give me plenty of time to take in any extra bulges.'

The man did as he was told. His erection was much stronger now, so although not massively well-endowed, he was confident there would be at least something that counted as a bulge.

He was also glad that he had changed into a pair of jeans. He felt certain that his oozing precome would be visible had he remained in his light grey suit trousers.

'Thank you. I can indeed pick out your erection,' she said. 'Is it uncomfortable, trapped inside those denims?'

'It's both uncomfortable but also very nice,' said the man.

'How so?' came the question.

'Erections like this tend to focus things very much on the base of the shaft which is where I am starting to feel a constant tingling now. I know it won't stop until I have a full orgasm.'

If only she knew how hard she had his juices flowing already! He had to divert for fear of actually blowing there and then.

'Are you wearing stockings?' he asked, seizing back the dominant role.

'Yes, I am,' she breathed softly.

'Please swing your legs out from under the bar, knees together, and straighten your skirt a little. Then with your hands show me where your suspenders are placed,' he instructed.

She did exactly as she was told, her hands coming to rest halfway down her inner thighs.

'Now, cross your left leg over the right and as you do so pull upward on your skirt so that I, and the whole room, gets to see just a suggestion of stocking top.'

Once more she did it beautifully, coming to rest in exactly the position requested and revealing an exquisite thigh in the process.

Having issued one command each, they were now locked eye to eye, pondering their next move. Both knew that this silence was also part of the game and neither felt uncomfortable about it, as would have been the case in a normal conversation.

The man was still dominant and eventually he spoke.

'I would like us to retire to your room now,' he said.

'OK.' She nodded. 'Any reason why mine?'

'There may be items there I want to see,' said the man.

'Of course, I wasn't thinking,' she said quickly.

'Before we do, we should take a couple of beers with us,' he said.

If she was confused or puzzled she didn't show it.

'Very well,' she said, content to remain submissive for the moment.

With that, the beers were procured and the couple eased themselves simultaneously off their stools and walked slowly toward the lift. They both knew that they had captured the attention of some of the other guests in the bar with the skirt-raising role play and they could feel the anonymous eyes on their backs. It only added to the tension that was now building between them. They were both very confident about this game now and knew it could go wherever they liked. Because either could end it whenever they wished, they both felt in control.

As they entered the lift, the man could contain himself no longer. 'Are you wet?' he asked.

'Tell me how wet you think I might or might not be,' she said, mischievously switching roles.

'It's my guess you've been a little wet all day since your orgasm this morning. Right now I would imagine you are even more so.'

'Dripping,' came the one-word answer as the lift found the right floor and they headed to the woman's room.

Once inside the man resumed the dominant role and instructed the woman to lie on the bed, pillows built up behind her back against the headboard.

'With your knees and ankles together just draw your legs upward so that your skirt falls on to the quilt. Keep your high heels on.' As if she needed telling!

She did exactly as requested, putting her beer on the side table, within reach.

The man moved a chair to the bottom of the bed and placed himself in it. Any movement of the woman's legs would now give him a direct view up her skirt and she, of course, knew it.

'Please take off your jacket and throw it to the floor,' he instructed. This done he could now focus on the woman's breasts and brassiere in full for the first time.

They were truly beautiful and his eyes lingered before issuing his next instruction.

'Please caress your nipples through your blouse and bra,' he said.

The woman brought her right hand to her left breast and did exactly as instructed. First she cupped herself and then rolled her nipple between thumb and forefinger, letting out a little gasp as she did so.

The man could see the nipple of her right breast hardening as she played on with her left, eyes closed, head back, but knees still together.

'Put your hand inside your bra and play with your nipple directly,' the man said. 'Tell me how it feels'

'Let me play a little first,' she said. The man liked this. She was still submissive but had sneaked in an instruction. She was so clever!

As she played she opened her eyes and resumed control.

'Unfasten those jeans, please. I want to see your cock.'

The man had no option but to obey, and it would be a welcome release for his constrained member but he was worried that he might just come too soon, such was the perfection of the lady before him.

He unbuckled and unzipped to reveal soaking underpants into which he delved for his scrotal sack, lifting out his balls and pushing his cock upward, hoping to make it look bigger.

'Your precome looks delicious,' she said. 'I so want to taste but I know I can't.'

'Not in this game,' he replied. It was his turn to be mischievous.

'We'll see,' she said, determined not to be outdone by any mind games.

'Take those jeans right down, please. Pants and jeans down to the ankles is how I want you,' she commanded, still caressing her breasts.

The man was happy to do it. But the tingling at the base of his shaft had been intense for a while now and he knew that any instruction to touch himself might bring the release he wanted to avoid, so he grabbed the initiative back.

'Unbutton your blouse, please, and let me see more of your breasts,' came the command.

The woman eased her hand out of her bra cup and dutifully unbuttoned to reveal an expensive white bra and a somewhat heaving chest.

'Now, lift up your skirt and let your knees fall apart.'

As she did so she revealed the full milky glory of her suspender-clad thighs. The man caught his breath, such was the magnificence of the sight, but within a second he couldn't breathe at all as his eyes searched for the woman's panties. There were none!

He could clearly see a gorgeous triangle of black hair sitting atop the outer lips of a truly soaking pussy, the juices flowing freely downward to the duvet cover, which any moment now was to be the recipient he so wanted his tongue to be.

His mind still racing, he flashed back to the bar earlier, before he had even spoken a word to this incredibly erotic creature. She had come to the bar with no panties on!

Gathering himself, he asked: 'When did you take off your knickers today?'

'I was still wet this morning from my orgasm and my panties were pretty soaked by mid-morning so I popped them off in the ladies' and went without,' she answered.

'You didn't want to put on a clean pair before you came to the bar?' he asked.

She paused. Realising that the game demanded the truth or it would be over, she said, 'I noticed you looking at me during check-in. I thought it might be fun to be without any panties if I saw you again later. It would be even more fun if we actually spoke to each other, which of course we did.

'Don't worry, I had nothing planned. I was just playing a game with myself more than anything,' she explained.

The man, totally taken aback, involuntarily pumped

another pulse of precome onto the head of his cock, which added to the reservoir already there, now flowing freely down his shaft.

'And as we spoke in the bar, your game was already underway then?'

'Yes.'

'That's why you stayed to chat. You wanted to know how it would feel talking to a stranger whom you knew found you attractive, whilst wearing no panties?

'That's right.'

'And how did it feel?'

'It's a great shame you didn't look at the bar stool as we left. There was a huge stain of my juices there as I got up. Goodness knows what the next person to use it would have thought,' she said innocently.

The man was speechless and happy to be so. He knew he was locked in a high-octane sexual vice with the most captivating woman he was ever likely to meet in his life and he wanted the moment to last. He had no wish to be dominant with her any longer. She was in charge and they both knew it was she who would decide exactly how their game would end.

'Is this going how you envisaged it?' she asked sweetly.

'Absolutely,' said the man. 'You have been incredible. I just hope I don't come too soon. I want this to go on a while.'

'Don't worry,' she said. 'I can see the state you are in. Concentrate on me if you wish. But I want your cock in full view still'

The man breathed a sigh of relief as he grabbed his beer and took a long draught. Gathering his thoughts, he feasted on the sight before him.

'Please unbutton your blouse and let me see your breasts.'

She did as instructed, revealing a perfect cleavage, her breasts rising out of their cups as she fondled her nipples delicately.

'Ease them out, please,' he went on. Once again she sublimely did as she was told, revealing deep, dark nipples, hugely erect between her fingers.

'What next?' she inquired.

'Do you want to come?' he asked.

'Very much so,' she said. 'This last 30 minutes has been amazing. I had no idea this could possibly happen. But it has, thanks to your fantasy.'

The man looked intently at the dark stain appearing on the duvet beneath the woman's crotch. 'You need to come badly, don't you?' he said.

'Will you allow me to play?' she asked.

'Did you pack a vibrator for this trip?' he asked.

'No. Not this time. Is that a problem?'

'Could you use the bottle instead?' he inquired.

'Why not?' she said, reaching over to pick up the beer bottle from the side table and slowly moving it down toward her oozing pussy.

Effortlessly, the neck of the bottle disappeared inside her vagina, pushing her swollen clitoris upward and outward into view for her solo audience.

The man wanted to speak but there was no need. She knew exactly what he was thinking and that she had complete control. She had taken over his game and would now lead him exactly where he wanted to go.

She eased the bottle a little deeper and angled it more prominently on to her clit, moaning just a little as she did so. She lifted herself up the bed and bucked down on the phallic instrument between her legs, this time gasping louder as her arousal started to reach a point of no return.

Once more her timing was perfect.

'Drink?' she enquired, slowly easing the drenched bottle from her pussy and offering it to the man.

How did she know to do that? He would never know but he would never forget the moment as long as he lived. He

199

stepped out of his shoes, socks, pants and jeans, took the offering from the woman and raised the bottle to his lips.

A heady aroma of alcohol and the sweetest pussy juices he had ever tasted completely engulfed him. As he drank, he drank her in her entirety. This vision before him had given him such splendid and cherished access to her very being that he was literally overwhelmed.

He sank to the side of the bed, sucking on the bottle as if for his very existence.

As he did so the woman let a finger slip deftly to her now swollen clitoris. She too had reached a stage in the game where the boundaries they were now crossing was becoming too much.

She stroked herself, slowly and purposefully, her breathing becoming faster and her moans taking their own course.

She had just enough presence of mind left to issue one last command through the torrent of pleasure coursing through her body.

'Bring that cock toward my mouth,' she gasped.

The man wrenched himself from his suckling of the beer bottle and, on his knees, brought himself into the position requested.

Moaning softly, she turned to face his dripping, rock-hard cock.

'Just let me know when,' he said, his hand gripping the shaft and moving the head within an inch of her mouth.

She was rocking on the bed now. Her knees up higher, her legs falling wider apart as she prepared to ride the wave.

When it started, she could only scream like a wild animal as every sensation in her body derailed her senses.

The man squeezed his shaft just once as she bucked her head back and, despite her convulsions, managed to look him straight in the eye as she accepted the first load of his huge ejaculation.

Uncontrollably he pumped again and again into her

200

mouth, maintaining the head just an inch from her lips as his semen ran down her chin and onto her breasts. She swallowed greedily, rubbing the remainder into her nipples with her free hand, the other still locked on her clit.

The man almost collapsed as the enormity of the orgasm and the whole situation took hold. They had enjoyed the most intense, intimate sexual experience imaginable and yet their only contact had been through his ejaculate.

He slumped and slithered to the floor. She closed her eyes and crumpled on the bed. It was over.

They both knew they could never, ever be as aroused again. Strangers just an hour earlier, now locked in an intimacy of the most private and unique nature.

No longer a fantasy. This game was their reality.

Date Night
by Ariel Graham

The first time I met him, he was looking for his wife's cat. The neighbourhood was new, and so were all the residents, and seeing we were a commute away from San Francisco and almost everyone seemed to drive into the city daily, after several months we were all still getting acquainted and learning names.

Mine's Charlene, but I didn't know his, and we'd been living a very short distance apart for a lot of months. What I did know was that he and his wife both worked, car pooled or park-and-ride shared with other groups, and kept late hours, barbecued on weekends, and didn't have any obvious kids.

Now I also knew they had a cat. That, or the male half of the couple was in serious need of therapy, because he was walking bent double, peering under cars and calling someone or something named Mr Chips.

I had just gotten out of my car and was unloading the groceries when Mr Chips' human came face to mid-thigh with me, and stopped dead. I watched the blush move up his face from the open collar of his chambray work shirt and thought I kind of liked it. The guy was dark, the kind of dark that shaves twice a day or ends up pirate-swarthy. He had light eyes and a chipped front tooth that showed when he grinned. I grinned back and stuck out my hand.

'Charlene Evers,' I told him. 'Please tell me you're

looking for a cat.'

His blush deepened a little. 'Cory Phillips. I think we're neighbours.'

'Definitely,' I said, nodding at our house. Tiny yard, cement walkway. The eaves on our houses almost touched, upstairs bedroom windows maybe 15 feet apart. 'Would you like a hand in looking for – was it Mr Chips?'

He looked even more embarrassed, if possible, which led me to believe it was his wife's cat.

'He won't come to anyone else,' he said, as if this were a failing on his, or the cat's, part.

'Really?' I handed him one of my grocery bags so I could rummage inside it. 'I have a way with cats,' I said, and produced a pop-top single-serve-sized can of tuna.

Cory laughed.

I put the can down mid-sidewalk and Cory called. About 30 seconds later a sleek black cat with white whiskers and a white moustache appeared from my back yard, looked at me with brief suspicion, ignored Cory and tucked into the tuna.

'And now he's eaten your lunch,' Cory said, stooping to pet the cat.

'No worries. Frees me up to have pizza.'

'I saw you talking to the neighbour,' Vince said when I went inside. He stood inside the living room, far enough back he couldn't be seen through the narrow floor-to-ceiling window next to the front door which comprised our entire view from the front of the house except for one lone window in what had become our spare room.

'You should have come out,' I said and plopped the carryalls on the counter. My job was to shop if we didn't want to live on potato chips and mac-n-cheese out of a box. His job was to put everything away.

Vince shrugged and stooped to give me a kiss. I brushed his blond feathery hair back and stood on tiptoe to meet him halfway.

'I liked watching the two of you together. You looked good, your blonde hair and him so dark.'

I grinned. I'd fallen half in lust with our neighbour on first sight but it was pretty obvious nothing was going to come of it. 'Don't get your hopes up,' I said. 'He nearly passed out from embarrassment just talking to me.'

I flipped the under cabinet lights on and started paging through a cookbook looking for something fast, easy and to which I had all the ingredients without going back to the grocery.

'So you mean it's unlikely he's going to be doing any of this?' Vince asked and came up behind me, slipping his arms over mine and reaching around to cup and squeeze my breasts. I let the cookbook pages rifle closed and leaned back against him. We could always get take-out.

'Mm, I don't think so.'

'How about this?' he asked, and ran his hands down the front of my body until he cupped my sex in his hand.

'Mm. Oh God. No. I think that would embarrass him.'

'Shame, that,' Vince said. He pulled the snap on my jeans, let the zip down and started tugging until my jeans and thong came down to my knees. He lifted me then, still facing the counter, and doubled me over the tile. One hand pressed down on the small of my back. The other dipped down and two fingers slid into me.

Vince moaned. 'You're so wet. I want to watch him do this to you.'

I felt him move slightly away and knew he was watching as his own fingers disappeared inside me, pretending someone else was finger-fucking me.

'Don't stop,' I said, and the hand on my back went away. I heard him fumbling wrong-handed with his own clothing and then he moved in close again, pushing his cock up where his fingers had been, moving my body so my clit ground against the tile, painful and intense. I arched up under him and Vince said, 'I just. Want to watch. Someone

205

else. Fuck you.' And came inside me even as I started to come.

Dinner ended up being pizza. Now I really was going to have to replace that tuna.

We went upstairs late that night, still content from pizza and sex, carrying our books. Vince went into the bedroom first so he could cross the dark expanse and turn on the bedside light rather than the overhead. I paused so I could turn off the hall light and was partway across the bedroom when he gestured me to be still.

'What?' I asked, though I dutifully froze in place.

'Come look.'

Across from us, separated by maybe 15 feet, Cory's bedroom was lit softly with candles. I squinted and an instant later I saw what Vince was watching.

Cory's cock was long and obviously very hard and he stood with his legs spread wide, in profile to the window, his head thrown back and one hand on his wife's head where she knelt, naked and golden, one hand cupping his balls as she sucked him off. Her other hand moved fast between her own legs.

I stood without moving, unwilling to look away, and felt Vince come up behind me, wrapping himself around me again. I was afraid to move, afraid we'd be seen, but Vince tugged my clothes, making me shift and turn within his grasp while across from us Cory's wife continued sucking and playing.

Vince got me naked and pushed me forward, just enough he could bend his knees, his long legs on either side of mine, and shove his cock hard into my cunt. I moaned, my own hands moving to find my clit as Vince reached around me to squeeze my nipples, and some movement we made caught Cory's attention. He stilled, frowning toward our window, and I wasn't sure if we were far enough back from the light that he'd see us but I tried to go still. Vince hadn't noticed,

206

maybe, and he took up a rhythm then, slamming into me and I looked away for just an instant. When I looked back Cory's head was thrown back, mouth open, his cock spurting on to his wife's breasts. She had her mouth open and her own hand had stilled, fingers probably still sunk deep inside herself.

I slipped over the edge, then, Vince coming hard inside me again, and when I looked up again, Cory's windows were closed, the curtains drawn.

For the next week I studiously avoided my neighbours. Vince, for all that he talks a good game and really would like to see me somewhere else with someone else, is shy. I didn't ask him about it, but he didn't say anything about Cory, so I figured he was doing a little subtle reconnaissance before leaving the house too. But just because I took care when going out to my car to drive to the humane society where I worked telling people that yes, little fluffy kittens did cost a lot to adopt, but look how *cute*, just because I watched on my way in and out of the house didn't mean I didn't look over at their bedroom windows every time I passed by ours.

Their curtains stayed closed.

'I'm going to be late tonight,' Vince said as we got ready for work a week after the inadvertent adventure.

That always sucks.

'How come?' Working at the humane society is a much easier dress code than working for an architectural firm. I was dressed long before Vince and sitting on the bed watching him.

'Just client meetings. Law firm wants to renovate a downtown building.' He stopped fussing with his tie – he couldn't tie them worth a damn and neither could I, so often he skipped it, got frowned at by the older partners but spent the day breathing easier – and came over to put his arms around me. 'If I found you naked and waiting when I got

207

home –'

I nipped at his chin. 'Been there, done that. Your ETA had no bearing on reality. I was cold, tired and doing a crossword.'

He nodded, remembering. 'We had boxed mac-n-cheese and watched a talk show. We *are* sexy.'

I laughed. 'Just call me if you're going to be too late,' and we both headed out.

I wasn't sure if it was my imagination but I thought he took a brief look around before he went outside.

Vince wasn't home when I got home, or when I finished doing a load of laundry or later when I pulled together everything we'd need for dinner, so I decided to take a run. Just after seven, it was still light and I ran along one of the green belts the city provided. Everyone said they were dangerous but there were so many joggers, runners, walkers, dog walkers, bikers, skaters and lovers that the only danger was traffic congestion, not being pulled into the foliage and attacked.

The sun was collapsing into a hot red disk over the Bay when I got back to our neighbourhood. I slowed half a block out, walking, and a few houses away I saw Vince. He always looked so good to me, tall and tanned and lean, sleeves rolled up to his elbows and the lanky, confident way he stood. I was about to call out to him when I saw he was talking to someone and I slowed. A few steps closer and I saw he and Cory stood talking. Both were in profile to me, Vince light and Cory dark, both tall and handsome. I thought about what Vince always wanted and shivered a little. Then I thought about what had happened a week ago and started thinking about crossing back to the far side of the street and taking a few more laps around the block until Cory went away.

Vince spotted me and called me over. 'You two have met, right?'

I'm blonde. I get red-faced when I run. At least they couldn't tell I was blushing. Probably. 'Nice to see you again,' I said. 'How's Mr Chips?'

'Arrogant,' Cory said and I noticed he looked a little red faced himself. 'Anyway, Vince, nice meeting you. Ten o'clock?'

'Ten o'clock,' Vince agreed.

'What's at ten o'clock?' I asked, and both men gave me blank expressions.

'I'll give the cat your regards,' Cory said and went away.

'Vince?'

He was already heading inside.

'Yes?' He held the door open for me.

'What's ten o'clock?'

'A time of day.'

'You're hilarious.'

'Can't help it.'

We'd stopped inside the doorway. Vince now gave me a long look. 'You look awful.'

'Thank you. And there I was admiring you when I got back from my run.'

'And Cory?'

I shrugged. 'I don't know if he likes admiring you or not.'

Vince rolled his eyes. 'You know what I mean.'

I winked. 'Fair play. What's at ten o'clock?'

'If you really want to know, you'll have to bribe me.'

I gave him a look. He unzipped his pants. I'm never averse to a bit of bribery. We moved off the tiled entryway and I knelt, drew his hard, thick cock into my mouth and nearly choked when Vince took up a very fast, deep rhythm. Something had him very happy to see me.

When he got close, I pulled back and grinned up at him. 'What's at ten o'clock?'

He looked at me with mock exasperation. 'Wench. Fine. Sex with the neighbours.'

And he slid his hard, straining cock back into my astonished, open mouth.

I pestered him through dinner, and cleanup, and during my own clean-up from my run, though eventually Vince just got tired of avoiding answering my questions and left the bathroom and left me to shower alone.

By eight o'clock I was a bundle of nerves. By nine o'clock I'd cleaned nearly everything in the house, even though I was wearing a pretty loose skirt and a tank top and no underwear per Vince's rather stringent suggestion.

Just before ten o'clock I'd decided it might be a good idea to pack everything we owned and move to another house. Vince's fantasy had been exciting as a fantasy. The reality a week earlier had been exciting as accidental reality. But tonight had a plan and Vince wouldn't tell me what it was. My heartbeat was loud and fast in my ears and I felt dizzy and off balance.

'And you call me the shy one,' Vince said as ten o'clock rolled around and we were still sitting alone in our living room.

I wouldn't have admitted it for anything in the world but I was a little disappointed that we were still home, and still alone together.

'I didn't know you knew I think you're shy,' I said.

Vince worked his way through my sentence and added, 'And you also consider me the unobservant one?'

Since he'd already tripped over several very apparent objects left out on the floor and asked me three times where his book was when it was on the coffee table in front of him, I thought I could nod at that one.

I didn't. I was still nervous. 'It's ten o'clock,' I said finally. 'After.' I nodded at the clock on the DVD player before I remembered it often ran fast.

'You're right. *Very* observant.' And he smirked, and held his hand out, and I swallowed and stood and took it, wondering.

He led me upstairs. There was something comforting knowing we were still in our own house. There was something wildly exciting about knowing the little I did – soon we wouldn't be alone in our house. Were they coming over? Were we changing and going over there? What had Cory and Vince agreed to?

And halfway up the stairs I thought I understood. Sex with the neighbours. We'd already had sex with the neighbours, hadn't we? And while maybe Vince hadn't watched Cory actually touching me, it had been *very good* sex between us that night.

The bedroom light was already on. The bedside lights had been moved and faced each other in the middle of the room, illuminating a spot directly across from the side windows. The back windows drapes were closed. The side windows drapes stood open, damp Bay air coming in the window and the low sound of voices from across the short distance between our houses.

Cory and his wife – Anna, Vince said she was called – stood framed in a similar glow of light within their own bedroom.

She was small and honey coloured, with a mane of hair and lips so glossed they glistened in the light. She wore a simple black dress with white buttons all the way down the front and she stood holding Cory's hand. Cory wore jeans, no shirt, his face well past its mandatory five o'clock shave. I wanted to bridge the distance between us and lick the coarse stubble on his chin. I wanted to run my fingers over his wife's breasts and tear the black dress from her.

But I couldn't touch them. So I turned to Vince and rose on tiptoe to wrap my arms around his neck and find his mouth with mine.

His mouth crushed my lips. He bit my lower lip and tugged. His hands found the hem of my dress and hauled it up. I felt cool air on my naked ass and Vince's hands, squeezing, long fingers pressing my flesh, lifting, moulding, mauling, separating. I moved a little, opened my eyes, and saw that Cory had unbuttoned Anna's dress down to her waist. Her breasts were as golden as the rest of her, with surprisingly pink nipples, hard and long. Cory turned her, trying to watch us at the same time he bit and licked. Anna's head fell back. She reached for him, fumbling with his jeans even as he pulled her dress the rest of the way open, showing us her slightly rounded stomach and shaved mons, the way she stood with her legs slightly apart, waiting for his hand or cock or mouth to find its way there.

I shuddered and tugged at Vince's shorts, even as he tangled me in my tank top, pulling it over my head, getting it into his face, laughing in joint frustration as we briefly blindfolded ourselves. And then we were watching again, watching as Cory knelt in front of Anna, his tongue working between her legs, her hands pressing and squeezing her own breasts, and Vince held me in front of him and a little to the side, my hand caressing his cock, his fingers spreading my juices.

At some signal I missed, or by some unspoken mutual agreement, we all stopped, both men crossing their respective rooms to bring back straight-backed chairs into the light and since the one in our room was one of our dining room chairs, I understood this had been arranged. Vince sat, and pulled me to him, turned me back to face the window where Cory and Anna had assumed the same poses. And then he pulled me down on his cock, his hands coming around to squeeze and play with my breasts.

'Spread your legs over mine,' he said, his voice hoarse, and I saw Anna straddling Cory, her sex splayed and Cory's cock sunk deep inside her. I threw my legs over Vince's and he pushed me forward, just enough so my shoulders moved away from him, my ass moved toward him and he sank deep into me, fucking me very fast.

***

We all came within minutes of each other. My usually silent partner made some kind of shout as he buried himself inside me and came. I don't think I made a sound, but Anna cried out Cory's name and Cory shouted something incoherent and I realised until then we'd all been mostly silent.

And stayed that way after. In the aftermath we sat, two plus two, wives still straddling husbands' laps, the four of us sweaty and dishevelled and sated, and stared at each other across the space between our houses.

Finally we all started moving and I expected someone to draw the curtains and that perhaps all four of us would be avoiding the others for quite some time. Instead, when Vince and I stood and started to turn off the lights, at least the rather stage lights the bedside table lamps created, we saw a naked and beautiful Cory come up to the window with a notepad. We could have heard him easily if he'd spoken and raised his voice even a little, but somehow communicating through signs was in keeping with the evening.

Cory's sign read, 'Same time next week?'

Vince grinned at me, then rummaged until he found an old sketch pad and a marker and wrote on the back, 'It's a date.'

Also from Xcite Books

Kinky Girls

Women who act on their most shameful fantasies and embark upon the most daring misbehaviour, is still the most enduring and timeless theme in erotic fantasy, and loved by male and female readers alike. And this collection takes the idea of a kinky adventurous woman to the max. A collection of 20 original, varied, outrageous, eye-watering and utterly sensuous stories from the best new voices and established authors around today.

ISBN 9781907016561   £7.99

Indecent Proposals

A kinky collection of erotic stories exploring sexy propositions and inappropriate behaviour in edgy situations. 20 brand new stories from the best new voices and established authors around today. Guaranteed to be surprising, inventive, imaginative and talked about. The first of four new Xcite collections in 2011 exploring the themes that worked so well for Black Lace.

ISBN 9781907016585   £7.99

Threesome

Threesome – When One Lover Is Not Enough is a collection of twenty varied stories with ménage themes. All combinations of couplings are explored allowing the reader to indulge in a fictional feast of ménage naughtiness.

ISBN 9781907016554   £7.99

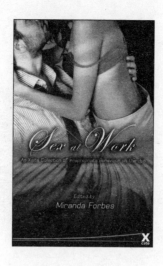

Sex at Work

Stationery cupboard trysts, conference connections and office party couplings – we all know that the workplace can be a hive of sexual activity.
In this collection Xcite have gathered together a selection of the best writing about inappropriate behaviour on the job.

ISBN 9781907016578 £7.99

Xcite Books help make loving better
with a wide range of erotic books,
eBooks and dating sites.

www.xcitebooks.com
www.xcitebooks.co.uk

Sign-up to our Facebook page
for special offers and free gifts!